D1552522

Afterimages

Stories

Marie France

Print ISBN: 978-0-57849-187-5

eBook ISBN: 978-1-54397-350-1

For Steve and Marina

Contents

Small Havens 1

After Roger 23

Little Turtle 45

The Pool Inside the Villa 71

Their French Mothers 93

ACKNOWLEDGMENTS 117

Small Havens

When they reached the entrance, Maxine slowed to make the tight turn, impressed with how the Chevy Tahoe held the curve. The driveway of the nursing home was so quaintly miniature, it was as though horses and carriages were still expected to arrive at what used to be an antebellum manor. The families that had farmed here for generations were gone now, replaced by a Vietnam veteran, recently deceased, and his Filipino wife, who had capitalized on the scenic property in the remains of the Northern Virginia countryside.

Mark got out of the vehicle first and came around to help his mother-in-law. She wouldn't budge, not until Maxine took one arm, and he the other. Once on her feet, Mum pushed back hard. At seventy-five, she remained athletic and strong after years of hiking. It was her dementia that had begun to progress at a certain clip. Two big orderlies came out to the parking lot then and tied her into a wheelchair. Maxine and Mark watched with a sense of surrender themselves as Mum succumbed to all that manhandling and allowed herself to be wheeled forward, slumped and silent, toward the entrance to her new home.

In the brightly lit vestibule, Catarina Hunt was there to greet them. Tall and slim, her hair was as long and glossy as a young girl's. The Japanese cast to her features must have made her pretty once, Maxine thought. Now a widow and the sole proprietor, Mrs. Hunt was said to run the facility with a "mother's touch." The staff came mostly from the Philippines, too, and were said to be attentive, which was why Maxine and Mark had chosen this long-term care facility for her mother, despite the distance.

Something there in the threshold set Mum off, probably the situation itself. She began to curse a blue streak. My God, she's acting like she's possessed. Maxine felt a rising panic. Mrs. Hunt didn't seem the least bit perturbed, however. Quite calm, she began to sing in a high incantation, which softened into a lullaby, as they proceeded into the main lobby. Her song was foreign. Tagalog, probably. They were fortunate there. Mum respected the folkloric. She bowed her head, as they wheeled her into the annex that gave the old house its modern purpose.

Maxine and Mark were determined not to let a week go by without visiting Mum. They took turns going out to the Hunt Home. Mark didn't mind. He was fond of his mother-in-law. They had science in common, he an eye surgeon and she a botanist. When he visited Mum, he arranged for the two of them to sit outdoors together in the garden patio and pore over *Curtis's Botanical Magazine*. Mum showed every sign of enjoying the illustrations and ran her hands over them, tracing the outlines of familiar plants. When Mark read aloud from the *American Journal of Botany*, however, or coaxed her thoughts on the latest in *Botany News*, she had nothing to say.

Each time Mark came out to visit, Mum seemed more puzzled than the last, her smile uncertain, as if embarrassed by her trouble placing him. He showed her a few recent photos of Shelley.

"Who's the pretty girl?" Mum asked.

She would have been proud to know her granddaughter had just received her degree in marine biology and was hired right away, part of a wetlands study down in Louisiana. Mum had been Shelley's early guide along the riverbed. How many hours, Mark wondered, had he watched the two of them pore over trays and trays of specimens.

The weather grew too cold to sit outside. More and more, Mark found reasons why he couldn't get out to see Mum. His wonderful mother-in-law seemed gone. Only her outer shell remained.

Once winter settled in, Maxine was the one who made the trek out there the most. She had grown to appreciate the long drive, and was in no hurry to arrive at her destination. It was piercing to be the last person her mother seemed to recognize. And it was unnerving to reckon with her stray intelligence, the residue of a mind that used to work so well. Once she left the highway, Maxine got a kick out of how well the Tahoe handled the gravel and took the sudden dips in the dirt roads.

Only Shelley's voice in her head spoiled the pleasure: "but you're emitting way more carbon than a regular car, Mom."

During college, when she came home on breaks, their daughter seemed to arrive on their doorstep magically unmussed by public transportation. On her shoulders lay her heavy hair and the straps of her backpack. There was no one Maxine would rather see. Even so, she didn't like being singled out as the bad guy, just because Mark was willing to settle for a Honda Accord.

After Maxine parked and entered the dementia unit, little coping mechanisms sprung up without much forethought. She would stop in the sunroom off the common area, which was her comfort zone. There she paused to collect herself among the stuffed animals. Snoopy, with his big, soft nose was a favorite. Sometimes she even dozed off for a few minutes before she headed down the hall to Mum's room.

On the drive home from the facility one afternoon, Maxine pulled into the parking lot of one of the big box stores that beckoned in spots along the highway. The setting sun had turned the sky lavender and pink as she headed into the brilliantly lit warehouse where every household prod-uct could be had, mostly in bulk. It was the toy section that attracted her. All the fluffiness came in soft pastels, and it was possible to buy a single unit. Back inside the Tahoe, Maxine set Hello Kitty beside her on the capacious passenger seat.

Alongside Kitty, she placed a bag of cheap chocolate candy, an impulse purchase at the checkout counter, which she snacked on all the way home.

To detour to a big box store after a visit to the Hunt Home was habit forming. Maxine craved the determined gaiety, the neon, and the bright colors after she left Mum behind. Pretty soon the backseat filled up with bunnies and bears, dogs and cats. Snoopy was a favorite, in a range of sizes and costumes. At a red light sometimes, she turned to look back at all those cuties. They cheered her up. The extra pounds she was gaining from the candy were the one bad side effect. She had sold her dance studio just before Shelley graduated from college this past May. After thirty years, she no longer started every morning at the practice barre. To dance now would be a reminder that her modest career had come to its end.

So join a gym, she told herself, as she crossed the parking lot to visit Mum on another cold, gray Saturday afternoon in March. Spring was slow to show itself this year. Shelley was home that weekend, and she and Mark had gone off to a lecture at the local community college. In the sunroom, Maxine sunk into the pale sofa with its faint food stains and dozed off almost immediately.

"Meditating, are we, dear?"

Maxine awoke with a start to Catarina Hunt's thickly accented English.

"My darling Maxine, I do so regret to disturb you. Yet I

have something I must tell you." Such a showy way she had about her. Maxine couldn't help but think of the hostesses who entertained men in Southeast Asia. Maybe that was how Catarina met her late husband. Today she wore a long, purple sheath with bursts of pink in the pattern. The colors sent Maxine back in time to her ballet studio, where she had helped five-year-old Shelley tie a pink scarf around her purple leotard. Her daughter had looked uneasy among the other little girls, whose leotards were black and who wore no scarves around their middles. Already it was clear that Shelley had no aptitude as a dancer and had taken no pride in being dressed like one. Yet Maxine had singled her out as an example. "Look at these colors, girls. They're what you'll see on stage. Worn by real ballerinas." Maxine had buried her disappointment, just as her own mother must have buried hers when Maxine had shown no interest in fossilized ferns.

Once they settled into her office, Catarina flashed Maxine a smile in gleaming red lipstick. "It's about your beautiful mother," she said.

"Oh? Is there a problem?"

"Well, yes, there is. She's perfectly fine, you understand. No worries there. I'm afraid it's something she's been a party to. Something she has done."

"What has she done?"

"Oh, nothing so terrible as all that. Except, you see, that it *is* terrible for *him*, you know. Your dear mother. She hit a nerve, I'm afraid."

Maxine shifted in the chair. "I'm sorry. Who are we talking about here, besides my mother?"

Catarina looked startled. "Oh my goodness. Why our Activities Director, sweetie. Raúl Marquez. I believe you've met him? We do introduce all of our staff to the families."

"I suppose I've met him, then."

"Well, let me refresh your memory, dear."

Through the office window, Maxine followed Catarina's finger as it pointed to a man, slight and small, who stood across the common area. Filipino, Maxine assumed. Of Chinese stock with a dash of Spanish, she guessed. His cheekbones pressed against his skin, remindful of a death's head.

"Raúl has worked out very nicely here as Activities Director," Catarina explained. Her voice was more relaxed and conversational now. "He runs the bingo and the bowling, and he really loves Twenty Questions and Test Your Knowledge. He already knew the names of all the U.S. presidents when he arrived here and the movie stars from bygone eras. Then he studied up on TV, the way one must."

"How nice." Maxine struggled to remain patient and polite.

"No, not nice. Not anymore, dear." Catarina heaved a heavy sigh.

"So what has my mother done to annoy him?"

"Oh, your dear mother," Catarina giggled. "Whom we all love so very much. And yet I must say. Oh dear, how best to put it?" She seemed to ponder as she drummed her long, red nails on the desktop. "Your mother was a bit too, shall we say, forward."

"Forward? What do you mean?"

Catarina bowed her head. "She talked dirty to him. Yes, she did. I am sorry to have to say so, but, there it is, the truth."

"I'm surprised to hear it." Politeness was one of the last of Mum's social graces to survive.

"Oh, she wasn't polite in this case. There was quite a scene, dear."

"Tell me what happened."

Catarina took a deep breath. "Oh, your sweet mother. She said bad words to Raúl so very loudly in a public place, the all-purpose room. And she said them more than once. Everybody was there for a birthday party. George Wilkes turned ninety-five."

"What did she say exactly?"

"My goodness. You really want to know?"

"Yes, I'd like to know, yes."

"Actually, dear. What she said was fellatio."

"Fellatio?"

" ... and cunnilingus. She said that word too." Catarina's voice trailed off.

"I see. That's all? Just the two words?"

Catarina's eyes went round. "Oh, they were quite enough for us." She hesitated and then went on. "Well, she did put two and two together, if you read my meaning. What Raúl should do to her, and she to him."

Maxine suppressed her smile. "Forgive me. But people here. Would they really comprehend?"

"Oh, you would be surprised, my dear. You would be surprised. You don't have to be a PhD to know those words. People know. They remember, they remember. And then of course the whole staff was there to witness."

Maxine gave Catarina a smile. "You don't see the humor in it?"

Catarina's return smile was no more than a reflex. "Oh, yes, *I* see. But, you see, Raúl doesn't. He's got all that baggage. The PTSD, honey."

Maxine must have looked blank.

"Torture. President Marcos was not a nice man. Raúl crossed him. You didn't need to be a big shot to get under Marcos' skin, sweetie. Raúl loved to teach his students about democracy, and I think, dear, that some of them liked what they heard enough to go out of the classroom to work for a new government."

"Well, I'm sorry my mother got under his skin," Maxine muttered.

"Your dear mother's behavior is part of a pattern, I'm afraid. She has been seen kissing the men out here, the ones in their wheelchairs who cannot defend themselves. She's been seen kissing their bald heads in long and deliberate ways, I've been told."

Maxine bowed her head. What dementia could do to a person. It was so terrible. She had always known her mother to be low key and rational, above all else. Where had she gone? Who was she now?

Catarina went on. "We do understand there's a reason for her behavior; that she needs to prove she's alluring to feel worthwhile, maybe even safe."

"Alluring?" How ridiculous. It was true that Mum had retained her good looks into her seventies, but there was no one more straightforward, no one less coy. She had spent her life in jeans and a tee shirt. She cut her own hair, for God's sake.

"Dementia can bring old demons to the surface, perhaps," Catarina said.

"Demons?"

"The sexual abuse. Your poor dear, darling mother."

"Sexual abuse? What do you mean?"

"Why, it's noted in her psychological profile. In her medical records, dear."

Maxine felt the shock pass through her body. "I never knew."

Catarina nodded several times in sympathy. "You have power of attorney now, though. You have a right to know."

"What does her profile say?"

"When she was a little girl, she was someone's plaything."

"Plaything?"

"You know. Someone's doll." Catarina sounded distracted, as if she were talking to herself. "Oh dear. For the life of me, I cannot remember whether the man was an uncle or a neighbor." She began to drum her fingers on her desk again. Then she refocused. "I am sorry, Maxine. The details are not fresh in my mind. My apologies. I will get the file for you."

"Well, what you say sounds just incredible." Maxine was angry now, wanting to come to Mum's defense. "She never acted like anything happened to her like that. She was strong. She was the soul of reason."

"Yes, I'm sure she was," Catarina whispered. "And still is," she added. "Her reason is just hiding from us now." She came around her desk and lightly draped an arm around Maxine shoulders. "I will go find that file."

The manila folder she handed Maxine was thick with Mum's medical history. Evidence of sexual abuse in childhood appeared in a brief notation in a gynecological report that dated back decades. Yes, the perpetrator was said to have been a neighbor. No details to recall, let alone to try and forget.

Silence filled the office. Maxine took comfort in it. Her poor mother. Who never told her. Who kept secrets. These were an affront to Maxine. Over the past few months, she had all but lost Mum. Had she ever known her in the first place? Never one to hug and to kiss; self-control was her signature trait. Always chill. Never surrender. Not to joy, not to grief.

Mum carried on as Mum always had. Then that reserve of hers got rammed into reverse, apparently.

Catarina broke into her thoughts. "You are quite right, you know, dear Maxine," she said, her voice softening. "It is going to take some time. Time to digest this news. I do so sympathize."

She bowed her head, with some ceremony, before she reassumed her ordinary posture, erect and regal in her swivel chair.

"Regretfully, dear, I must draw your attention back to the problem we do have to solve. You see, Raúl will not stand anymore in the center of the all-purpose area and speak out very loudly, the way one must on account of all the deafness, dear. No, no. He will not do that while staff members stand at the edge of the room to see if your sweet mother will embarrass him again."

Maxine crossed her arms against her chest. She felt embarrassed herself, aware of how her jeans hugged her thighs, her sweater cupped her breasts. She would dress with more care when she came out here in the future.

"Yes, but couldn't this man, Raúl, make allowances?" she asked. "You know, show the compassion that one damaged person can feel for another?"

"Oh, I'm surprised to hear you say that," Catarina exclaimed. "Good for you, dear. Oh, that's so good of you to think." She clapped her hands. "The Holy Spirit is with you."

Her excitement died away quickly, though. "Only I'm

afraid that Raúl isn't as strong as he once was, dear. I don't think he'll ever recover from what happened to him in prison. And now another humiliation. On account of that incident with your mother, whom we all do love so very much. Even so."

She paused then, letting the wall clock tick away before she spoke again. "So I was thinking, dear."

Her eyes met Maxine's.

"Maybe you could consult with your husband."

"My husband?"

"Yes. He is a doctor after all. If he were to find a new situation for Raúl, your husband would very much be doing some healing."

"A situation?" Maxine sat up straight.

"A job, a position. Raúl needs to pay his rent. He needs his dignity even more."

Maxine felt put out. Not ambushed, exactly, but put out. "If Raúl were a nurse," she began. "Or if he had any kind of a background in medicine or health care."

"Oh, there must be something your kind husband can do. He is so clever, I believe." An expectant look appeared on Catarina's face, and once again she let the silence settle in around them.

All right. Ambushed. Maxine had to admit it. "I'll talk to Mark."

"Wonderful, dear." Catarina sat back and sighed. "I

feel certain that you two will do something wonderful for Raúl's sake."

Maxine doubted it. She offered to talk to Mark only to put an end to this conversation. Mum wasn't responsible for her own behavior anymore, let alone this man's welfare. Neither were they. Were they? What exactly had they signed on to in all those papers they filled out before Mum could come live out here? Mark would know. He was a careful reader of documents.

An hour later she pulled into the driveway feeling queasy. On the passenger's seat lay an empty cellophane bag. She had eaten all of the chocolate kisses, unaware of having eaten anything at all. In the kitchen, Mum's elderly English terrier with the odd name of Herbert gave her a polite if subdued welcome. He knew better than to expect her to take him out for a stroll. Mark was his friend. After Mum had gone out to the Hunt Home, her pet had been in need of assisted living, too. In their empty nest of a house, Herb now had a room of his own, because Mark had said a dog could add so much to life. Maxine wasn't so sure.

Thirty minutes later, she was huddled over a cup of tea when Herb leapt up at the sound of the Honda. He trotted down the hall to greet her husband and daughter, home from their lecture. Shelley's voice floated into the kitchen in a lecture of her own. Marsh dieback. Low-oxygen water. The size of the Gulf's dead zone. The effect on waterfowl and fish. "As the climate warms, we'll need more wetlands, not less," she was telling Mark.

Her voice made Maxine's head throb. As her family entered the kitchen, she plugged her ears with her fingers. "I'm not listening," she said.

Shelley paused in her litany and looked at her mother curiously, as if she were another natural specimen to be assessed. "You look like a little girl, Mother, with your fingers in your ears like that."

"Not another word about carbon footprints," Maxine snapped. "I don't live in a third-world country, and I'll be damned if I'll act like I do."

Shelley looked stricken. Her voice dropped to a sad murmur in reply to her mother. "If you could see it down there." The litany began again. "The plummet in the bird population. The devastation to the trees."

"I told you, I don't want to hear about it." Maxine felt sickened by what she heard, despite her deep resentment.

"But you do like trees," Shelley persisted. "Remember?"

"People just want to be comfortable." Maxine struggled to regain her cool, the better to confront her rational daughter. "And you think it's a crime."

"No, I don't." Shelley sighed. "I think it's a shame. A tragedy."

They stopped. Because Mark asked them to stop.

On Sunday morning, mother and daughter embraced. Maxine felt sad to see Shelley go. Yet she felt some relief, too. Their differences of opinion took their toll. It was only a matter of time before Shelley would start in on them to sell their nice, big house and move into some shoebox of a condo.

From the kitchen window, Maxine and Mark watched as their daughter pulled out of the driveway. Shelley had bought a car, necessary to get around rural Louisiana. Naturally hers was an EV.

Once she arrived at her destination, she texted Mark to let them know. "Just between us, all those stuffed animals worry me," she added.

Mark gave a wry smile that his daughter couldn't see. "Why? Your mother has made good use of all that space in her SUV."

"So you're not worried?"

"Nah. They soothe her, I think. All those plush toys make her feel cozy."

At dinner Maxine told Mark about her conversation with Catarina out at the nursing home.

"Mum had an outburst. She upset a staff member with PTSD. Catarina thinks you could find the man another job."

Mark grunted in reply. The surprise came when he sat down and wrote out a fat check to the Hunt Home as if it were a prescription.

Maxine was livid. "You're taking the easy way out, Mark. I hate to see you cave."

"I just want to make sure your mother is well taken care of. There's nothing wrong with making a contribution to support the facility."

Maxine shook her head, disgusted. No, nothing was simple, not even easygoing Mark. She couldn't bring herself to tell him about the gynecologist's note in Mum's medical records. He had always been protective of her mother. Was it possible he sensed some wound she carried long before she lost her wits? Why darken his memories with a long-ago trauma Mum had kept from them anyway.

Maxine couldn't bring herself to make her weekly trek out to see Mum, either. She wasn't ready to run into Catarina, soon to be in receipt of Mark's extreme generosity. A late March snowstorm gave her an excuse to stay put, although the Tahoe would have made the trip possible. The first signs of spring were beginning to show themselves when a sense of obligation set her out on the road again to visit the Hunt Home. Mum seemed about the same. These days, her dull-eyed lack of recognition extended to Maxine.

On the way out to the parking lot, she spotted Raúl in a corridor. He was cleaning the floor, a mop handle in one hand and a pair of wooden rosary beads wrapped around the other.

Maxine stopped by the office.

Catarina came around her desk to embrace her. "You've been so kind, so generous."

"You have my husband to thank, not me. He's the soft touch," Maxine said, as flatly as she could. "I see Raúl is still here."

"Yes, yes," Catarina nodded vigorously. "How difficult it is to find a job out there in the US of A. Yet all is well," she added brightly. "Raúl is so happy, so happy, to stay on here and to take care of the chapel, to help the priest prepare for Mass. Nearer to God, if I may say so."

"What, he's no longer worried about sexy outbursts? His PTSD is in remission?" Maxine wanted to keep her cool but didn't.

"Dear, dear Maxine," Catarina murmured. Her voice purred, and her eyes were as watchful as a cat's. "You don't need to worry. Raúl feels safe again, out of the limelight. Many of our residents fail to recognize him, now that he no longer leads them in activities. As for your husband's gift, rest assured. His generosity is put to good use. Good use indeed. We're one family here. We all give, and we all receive."

Maxine's mind wandered. She had no way to gauge the truth here. What mattered was that Catarina was on notice: Maxine wasn't going to turn a blind eye just because Mark had been indulgent. She rose to leave.

Catarina stood up, too, slim as a taper. Her silver bracelets slipped down her forearm as she reached across her desk for Maxine's hand. "The Mass starts in ten minutes. Won't you join us this evening? You'll feel much fortified, dear. I feel certain."

Maxine hesitated. If the look in Catarina's eyes could be believed, her invitation was sincere. What possessed this woman? She ran a good facility, despite everything. By all accounts, she was a pillar in the surrounding community. Yet Maxine thought it wise to remain wary and watchful.

She and Mark were well aware of the Catholic Masses said in Tagalog out at the Hunt Home. Dozens of Filipino immigrants would show up to worship in what seemed to be intense and ritualistic ways. Yet the two of them agreed there was no need to object to the mumbo jumbo on offer, given Mum's dementia and her stout atheism.

What surprised Maxine this evening was that she felt inclined to attend the Mass. The thing was, she was getting too fat, and the Tahoe was getting too full of stuffed animals. A Mass might help her break her shopping habit, at least this once. She followed the worshippers, streaming in from the surrounding community, and squeezed in among the small bodies that stood along the back wall of the so-called chapel, a repurposed front parlor dating back to the house's antebellum days.

The priest strode in from a side door. Raúl followed and lit two tapers at either end of the makeshift altar. The frankincense was overwhelming, but soon enough Maxine's attention was drawn elsewhere, toward the light at the end of the tunneling blackness, shed by a congregation's worth of votive candles. Their warm-yellow flames jumped and waved, captive as they were within jars; some red, some blue.

Maxine shut her eyes and listened to the murmured call and response of the prayers, the meaning lost to her among all the voices disembodied in the dark.

"May I remind you that we are husks?" A man up front rendered the priest's question into English, which startled Maxine, and she opened her eyes.

"Those flames in the glass jars signal as much. Soon they will gutter and go out, with only a wisp of smoke to show for themselves, dim symbols of the dazzling light that is eternal. What remains are our souls."

Maxine glanced over at the candles. One of the flames caught her eye, one that danced among the other votives like a young girl. A bit frightened, she wanted to turn away, but the little-girl flame caught Maxine up and enveloped her within a far greater light than her immediate own. In this embrace, there might be love. Yet were she to hold me too close, I might burst into flame, husk that I am. Maxine shut her eyes again until the benediction, and the Mass ended. The lights came on, and the crowd of people stirred and milled about to greet one another.

"Thank you for coming, my dear." Catarina clasped Maxine's hand, with a searching glance.

Someday these visits will end, Maxine thought, as she drove away. Someday Catarina would call and say, "Your dear mother, whom we all love so very much. Even so." Meanwhile, you could write Mum off as out of order, on her way to flat lining. To nothingness. But there were mysteries, weren't there. Catarina and her cabal of Filipino Catholics believed in the soul. When Maxine pondered the whereabouts of the spirit that her mother still possessed, her mind leapt to Herbert, Mum's dog. Sometimes it seemed that some invisible bond of energy linked Mum to that animal of hers, that some cross-fortifying pulse enabled each of them to live on. Whatever the case, Mum and the defenseless little girl she used to be were safe with Maxine, whose love gave them a small, temporary haven from the eternal and its cloud of mystery.

As she hit the highway, her thoughts turned to her own little girl. Shelley was six again, and the homework was to draw to the sound of Rimsky-Korsakov's "Scheherazade." For once Shelley turned to Maxine for assistance. This wasn't science, it was fantasy, and Shelley felt as much at sea as Sinbad, unable to imagine how to draw anything that resembled what she heard. Maxine pulled a few crayons out of the box. She put her hand over Shelley's, and together they traced the sound in blues and greens and yellows. With a red crayon, Maxine had made a checkmark. "That's one of her feet dancing. Now you make one," she said, turning the crayon over to her daughter. One red vee after another, they traced the footwork of the great storyteller in the seraglio.

As she sped along the highway, Maxine's memories of her young daughter softened her up enough to shift forward to the present. Somehow she found she could allow Shelley's adult voice free rein. Once she was willing to go that far, it wasn't too difficult to imagine what her daughter wanted to say: "climb down out of the arms of your big SUV, Mom. Stop guzzling gas to drive out there and mourn the loss of Mum's mind all the time. Find a fresh, green way to rejoin the living."

Maxine shot past every strip mall.

On a Saturday morning, not long after a spring rain left every living thing in a state of sparkling lushness, Mark texted Shelley. He had news.

"Guess what? Your mom has started walking Herb in the morning."

"You're kidding. Imagine Mom communing with a real dog."

"Yes. Well, she is trying to lose some weight she put on this winter, but I still think she's starting to like Herb."

"A dog adds so much to life. Isn't that right, Dad?"

"Let's see what comes. I'm feeling hopeful at any rate."

"Yes, feel hopeful. Maybe one of these days you guys will even downsize."

After Roger

A nick in time, Roger had called it: the coastal slash that let the sea cut in and wash against the base of rock beneath the house. The water cut the property off from two more rounded rocks that lay a few hundred yards out. Except at low tide, you had to swim across or take the rowboat to reach these petite formations, each with a few stray pines to nurture, huddled against the sky. The two men had loved these islets. Two grace notes in the Maine seascape: these were the "girls" they admired from their front porch. On this first morning of his return, Walter preferred to look east, toward the ocean, whose impression of timelessness took the edge off death's part in life and simply let him be. His body relaxed and his bones settled into the rocking chair, which had survived, despite his neglect to stow it away at the end of last season.

For decades here in this venerable saltbox, they had held court, Walter and Roger, June through September. Walter's grandfather had built the house into the outcropping with a wraparound porch but no insulation and no heat source other than the fireplace in the front room. Granddad had wanted to enjoy nature, not to embellish a vacation home.

Last summer the cancer began to gain on Roger. By July, he was spending most of the day on a cot in the front room, near the screen door that led out to where Walter sat now. If Roger kept his eyes shut, he told Walter, the gulls sounded sharper in his ear. The irritation of their screeches actually brought him joy, still so good to be alive. Yet it seemed to Walter that it was the quiet that had done the most good, without the usual houseguests and parties. Under the cotton blanket that Walt spread over him, Roger slept and slept. One whole, last summer they were allowed. Well, there even were a few parties.

In October, the trek back to town had been an ordeal. At the apartment, they found they were locked out of their former lives. Pain invaded, and so did drugs. Home-hospice morphine dribbled into Roger's veins. In a drowsy voice, he spoke his fears. In November, he whispered that his stage fright was gone, and Walter braced for the phenomenal performance that would hurl his dearest companion out into the unknown. Only Roger slipped away, like a flat leaf on some small stream, whose flow Walter sensed but wasn't privileged to see. He had felt release, though, from the excruciation of their last stand.

Routine helped guide and support him in the months that followed. The apartment, now a dead zone, remained a convenient place for Walter's students to learn how to play piano and bass. They breathed life into the place all winter and provided a distraction. As spring gave way to summer, there came the tug of another routine, the annual return to the Maine house. Old times up there were well preserved. Nine months out of twelve, layers of memory lay undisturbed. For the first time, they attracted him, no longer so many dust bunnies to sweep away in favor of the here and now and then on to the future. There wasn't much here and now, much less a future, Walter thought, just a dead past. But in Maine, the past would feel different. Within the new, solitary atmosphere, feathery essences might float. If no soft shred of his lost love caught hold of him and clung, then maybe some cosmic kick in the shins would occur and revive him instead. Yes, he was in need of revival.

And so he had returned to their house in Maine. Life up here couldn't be what it once had been, of course. Still, he could pretend a little, couldn't he, and imagine that Roger lay just the other side of the screen door, breathing the same air. The pretense was painful, though, and he got up out of the rocker to begin the round of small chores to settle in for the season. In the driveway, he lifted out the big box of groceries from the trunk of the car. As he climbed the back stairs, he heard a telephone ringing. It was the old landline, which had hung on the kitchen wall forever.

"I'm not far away," Russ said. "I can get over tomorrow morning if that's an okay time."

Walter hadn't set eyes on his brother in many years. Then,

this past April, there he was: tall and thin, with the pale, fine features the two of them shared, heading down the center aisle of the church squeezed between buildings within a city block.

Why, Russ must have heard us, Walter realized. The quartet he belonged to had just finished the piece he had written as a coda to Roger's memorial service. The realization filled him with pleasure, although he knew better than to think Russ would appreciate the music. The brothers were born two years apart, but the differences in their dispositions had always been too stark to lead them into the usual sibling rivalry let alone friendship. Their parents were analytical people, who had not merely named their two sons. They had peered deeply into their psyches to identify each child's unique inadequacies from the start, some fifty years ago. Russ, they complained, was a pill, moody and sullen, with a head only for mathematics. Walter they dismissed as theatrical, his love of music the sign of a lightweight. Blessedly, their parents had paid for his lessons, although they never wanted to hear him play.

Siblings weren't consigned to their childhood roles forever, though, were they? In Walter's mind, the question had been a hopeful one as he watched his brother walk toward him across the stone floor of the church back in April. In this hour of my need, Walter remembered thinking, Russ was showing up. Water from some unknown source must be sweeping in across the empty, intervening years between us. Walter could almost feel the surge, because this water formed no barrier. It was going to lift them up and carry them forward, to bind them in a way they had never been. Viola bow in hand, he rose out of his chair. With his free hand, he grabbed hold of his brother's shoulder. "Russ," he cried. "It's great of you to come."

Russ had stood perfectly still, while all around them, the other members of the quartet were packing up to leave. "What are you going to do with the house," he asked, "the house in Maine?"

Walter had blinked and let his hand slide away from his brother's shoulder. "I have no idea," he said, in genuine surprise.

"Good." I want to talk to you about it." Russ's smile had looked pained. The look in his eye was intent; neither friendly nor unfriendly.

"Let's talk later." Walter had kept his voice bright, upbeat, to hide the plummet in his feelings to find Russ just as abrupt and remote as ever. "Once I'm up to it," he added, apologetic as ever to placate his sullen brother.

Russ did surprise him then. He gave Walter a light tap on the shoulder with the memorial program he had rolled up like a scroll. "My condolences," he said with a slight bow of his head. "The music was beautiful," he murmured, before he turned away toward the narthex, which led out to the street.

Why had he asked after the house? Walter had wondered as he watched his brother go. Russ had sold his half-interest in it years ago.

Now here he was again, just as summer was about to begin, calling the very house itself, pressing to meet. "See you tomorrow then," Walter said and hung up. He could hardly say "no, don't come."

Tires skidded on the gravel drive as the pickup pulled in fast the following morning and braked to a halt just shy of the back stairs. Russ always had been a speed demon. As he got out of the truck, so did a woman. At the top of the stairs, Russ introduced Vivian, who looked to be about forty, and thus maybe fifteen years his junior. The first wife had been petite, with a soft, rounded body. This one was blonde, as thin as a knife blade.

On the side porch they all sat down at the table that Granddad had made out of pine. It was here that the two men used to eat when they were children. A big family breakfast was one of many daily rituals, most of them puritanical in their rigor. Now the three of them gulped air, full of salt and pine, along with coffee Walter had brewed. Russ went straight to the point.

"Vivian and I: we'd like to build here. We don't have anywhere else to go. We don't have the money."

Russ had been on the road his whole adult life, as far as Walter knew: he was some sort of civil engineering consultant in the third world, which sounded well-paid enough. Why didn't he have money?

Russ filled him in: "Vivi's kids and my ex ate it all up. School loans, detox centers, alimony. Nothing that turned out worthwhile. We could have burned our dough. Same difference."

Vivian said nothing. She seemed like the kind of person who thought life was a bitch but was going to be a good sport about it. Still, she glowed with health, unlike Russ, who was haggard this morning, unshaven and uncombed in an old pair of jeans, looking at least as old as he was. The red leather clogs were a dash of panache. Somehow he had the money for expensive footwear at any rate.

"We want to build an addition," Russ went on, "with plumbing and HVAC so we can live here year round."

"Don't you work overseas?" Walter poured more coffee into each mug with a steady hand, proud to hide the fact that Russ had rattled him.

"My contract wasn't renewed. I ran into some trouble. Allegations." His voice died.

"Allegations," Walter picked up, "of what?"

"Sex crimes," Russ told him, always the straight shooter. Always impatient with euphemisms or any attempt to finesse the facts to spare anyone, even himself.

His arrogance always had been his strength, Walter thought, with some envy, and this attitude allowed him to brazen his way through situations that would embarrass many other people. Walter's own shock must have shown, though.

"Oh, for God's sake," Russ snorted. "It's a load of crap.

These things happen all the time out there. Local women come on to you. And then they spring their trap. They accuse you of unwanted advances: trumped-up charges, which they settle, once you pay up. Their own men put them up to these schemes too. The problem is, sometimes they kick up enough dust to leave a cloud that hangs over you bureaucratically. I tried to clarify the record, put it all behind us, when we flew to New York in April."

"So that's why you showed up," Walter said.

Russ looked blank.

"At the memorial service."

"Oh, yes," Russ said, nodding at the reminder. "I had seen the obit and thought I'd stop by to pay my respects and maybe broach the subject of our Plan B, which you weren't ready to hear under the circumstances. But I was in town that morning, anyway, meeting with the program office, making one last-ditch effort to try and salvage things. I got nowhere. Too near the end of our shelf life, I guess. Not young or brilliant enough to make exceptions for."

"You and Vivian?"

"Oh, she wasn't directly involved, of course," Russ said dismissively, "but Vivi knows the score: how these things play out in the developing world—so-called," he added, with the derision in his voice that Walter remembered well from their youth. Then Russ turned to her as if to coax her to speak.

She gave Russ a quizzical look but spoke readily enough. "Sexual exploitation by aid workers: it's a problem, yes, but also a scam. The chance for a local woman to make quick money is just too tempting. And then there's simple misunderstanding. It's not easy to interpret signs and signals and all the more so in another culture."

"Which makes it easy to cry rape," Russ jumped in to say.

"Yes, so I've heard," Walter said. He didn't want them to think they needed to talk down to him, the little brother with the sheltered life. Yet he was curious. "How did you come to work for the U.N.?" he asked Vivian.

"I didn't," she said. "Russ and I met in Ghana. One thing led to another."

Russ gave a rare smile. "We met ten years ago. I was under contract on a bridge project in the Volta Region." He turned toward his wife, clearly attracted to her.

What Walter found attractive was her poise, so different from his brother's restive presence across the table. "What took you to Ghana?" he asked her.

"I grew up there," she answered, "My parents were missionaries, Baptists from Texas."

Russ cut in again. "I helped her shake off that old-time religion."

"Your brother saved me from a dead end," Vivian agreed. "I'm no evangelist. Voodoo is more authentic in that part of the world anyway."

"Vivian is good with the locals," Russ said. "They call a lot more of the shots than they used to. That's fine, as it should be, but let's not forget. We did build a few good things in our time."

"Here, let me clear the table," Vivian said, and stood up in her brisk way. "Then we can roll out the plans."

"Plans?" Walter asked.

"Yes, we have an architect," Russ said. "He's been out here. We brought the blueprints along, so we can show you exactly what we have in mind. Why waste time and have you worry. It's going to be beautiful."

Did his brother really think he was being considerate, Walter wondered. He picked up the coffee pot and headed into the kitchen.

Russ followed on his heels. "Wow, get a load of this," he said and whistled. "Granite counters. What would Granddad say?"

"All the improvements were Roger's doing," Walter told him.

"And yet you never winterized," Russ said, frowning.

"Russ, the plans are still on the back seat," Vivian said. "Will you go get them?

Bring in my sweater, too, please."

It gave Walter some satisfaction to watch Russ go fetch for his wife. He had rarely seen him answer to anyone. Alone now with Vivian, she surprised him with a request to do something for her too: "Will you show me around?"

The living room was almost as spartan as when Granddad had lived here. Roger's improvements had taken place primarily in the kitchen and in the added bathroom. Vivian drifted over to the lithographs of old world concert halls and opera houses at the turn of the last century. Nothing else besides the shadows of the trees decorated the walls.

"How arcane," she said, and stared at the prints as if they were a great puzzle. "Is that the right word?" She seemed to be talking to herself rather than to Walter. "At least for me, they're rare, these drawings."

The lithographs weren't rare. But the facades of the buildings pleased Walter, because their doorways led to music, and music not only was the food of love but near to the essence of life as far as he was concerned.

"Do you like music?" he asked her.

"Well, that's a good question," she said, and folded her arms across her chest. "I was brought up on Baptist hymns and African rhythms. I doubt I would know any of the music that was played in these old buildings."

"Not Brahms, not Bach, not even Beethoven?"

"The 'Three Bs,'" she smiled, "would be pretentious, maybe even neocolonialist, in the world that Russ and I live in."

Walter nodded. "So we move in different sound circles."

"Yes, but I'm an easy listener. Who isn't? I might hear music like that in a hotel lobby and like it without even knowing I did." She turned back to the lithographs. "These I do

know I like. I'll keep an eye on them from my sleeping bag."
She winked. "We're going to camp out here in the living
room this winter. Did Russ tell you?"

"You do like to tease, don't you, Vivian?"

"Well, funny things do go on," she said, again as if to herself.

They moved on, and the lithographs passed out of view.
As they reached the staircase, she stopped to examine the
carved newel post at the foot of the bannister. "Oh, even this
is beautiful," she muttered. Roger had hired someone to strip
off the layers of paint to reveal the black walnut. "Can we go
up?" she asked.

Walter led the climb to the hallway, which ran the length
of the second floor. To open the bedroom door would be
intolerable. The spare room he didn't mind. Glass-front
cases held musical scores and librettos and sheet music;
American jazz artists mostly. Some of the paper had begun
to yellow. Nothing here of great value, except memories of
pleasurable jams with other musicians. One cabinet held
some prized record albums, neatly filed in slots.

Little Wayne found his way into Walter's head then. "Hey,
how you doin', man?" his voice rounded by delight. So many
times he had called the tune out of that old sax, which stood
over in one corner, while Walter had thrummed the bass
in the other. He had brought the instruments along from
the apartment this summer, just as he always had, because
you never knew when music might go ahead and bob to
the surface.

Thirty years ago, Walter played bass and sometimes piano in the smaller clubs that dotted Manhattan. In ever-shifting combos, inevitably he met the musician whose sound was reminiscent of the great saxophonist and brilliant improviser, Wayne Shorter. The resemblance was strong enough to earn him title to the "little" namesake. Little Wayne was also a piano man and no coke head, facts which had drawn the two closer. Walter was known as the monk, not for any resemblance to Thelonious but for his austere style, his one-cigarette, one-drink regimen. Walter had loved Wayne, not sexually so much, but for his sweet nature and for that creamy sound he brought out of the sax and later the keyboard after he folded rock and funk, bebop and blues into a jazzy blend.

Once Roger came into Walter's life, everything changed, almost all to the good. Tall and lean, Roger had been physically beautiful, financially successful, and socially commanding. Walter never understood what Roger saw in him. A whole lot of love was basically all he had to offer this man who welcomed him totally into his world but didn't much care to enter his. So Walter had left the music scene and began to teach mostly teenagers how to play the double bass, bowed for the orchestra or plucked for jazz. That was when he had begun to collect the sheet music and old scores that mapped out his own private universe.

Vivian moved from one display case to the next and scanned the contents. "All this paper and it's meant to be heard." Her voice was softer now, and the shift in tone seemed to signal a shift in mood.

Walter felt called to confide. "I can hear the sounds. Want me to sing out a few bars of something?"

"Oh, no," she said, and slowly shook her head. "I don't think I could handle anything that amazing, at least not yet. But thank you for sharing this trove of yours with me."

"My pleasure." In truth, he was sorry to see her retreat and no note sung.

For a moment they were silent. Then he listened as her voice found its way back to its usual register, light and ironic. "For me, this is all pretty heady," she said. "It's like a champagne brunch after a lifetime of rice and beans."

"You might get to like champagne," he said to her, and closed the door behind them.

Out in the hall she began to muse again on some counterpoint of her own. "A lot can resonate out of earshot. Sometimes we duck below our own radar. You know?"

"Sure, we tune out, if that's what you mean."

"I was thinking about what happened in Cameroon. You know: where Russ was accused of hanky-panky. He probably did do something; maybe something pretty bad; maybe not for the first time. The thing is, though, he's innocent in his own world. He doesn't get it when he's guilty in someone else's. Call him out all you want, he'll never believe it. He protects his mind from himself."

"Do you care about him?"

She hesitated, then looked up at him, doubt in her eyes. "Yes and no—which is to be expected—don't you think?"

"I don't think as much as you do, Vivian," he said, as gently as he could.

She nodded, thoughtful, and stoic, too, it seemed. "For such a long time, we lived these certain lives. And now we don't have to anymore. In fact, we can't."

Russ called up the stairs. "Come down and see our Plan B."

Walter watched his brother spread the blueprints on the big pine table. They were of no interest to him. He understood their impact already.

"Okay, so don't look at them," Russ said and pushed them aside. "But sit down, would you, and let me tell you how we see things." He motioned to Walter to take a seat in one of Granddad's chairs. "This place never interested me." He swung his long arm to take in the house and the surrounding scenery. "You know that."

Walter agreed. "Yes, you cashed out a long time ago."

"At a low point, yes," Russ said, sounding impatient, testy.

He didn't like to hear from the peanut gallery, Walter recalled.

"When we got back to the states last spring, we came up here to take a look around. Vivi wanted to see the place. She was curious, because frankly I used to brag about the property." Here he stopped to shake his head and grin. "A rolling stone has to impress somehow, doesn't he?

"That visit changed everything. I saw this old house in a totally new and positive way—through her beautiful eyes. So then I had to break it to her. You owned the house now. To live here, we had to get you to go along. Vivi said something amazing then. She said you weren't as considerate as you should've been."

"I wasn't?"

"You should have lent me money rather than take my share of the house."

"Russ, what's the idea?" Vivian called back to him. She had stepped away from the table to stand near the cluster of white pines, some of whose fragrant branches rested on the porch railing.

"You said it, Vivian, remember? And you were right. I was going through a divorce. It wasn't cool of him to do that."

"I didn't take your share," Walter said. "You asked me to buy you out, and I did. Even then, the sum was considerable."

"Roger bought me out, you mean," Russ said, dismissive. "There's something not quite right about that."

"There isn't?"

"No, there isn't. To buy me out with someone else's money so you could benefit from my misfortune. 'He brunches, while we live on rice and beans.' Isn't that right, Vivi? Remember?"

Vivian slapped on a smile, but it looked more like a grimace. "Yes, but we're here now. We can make everything work out, can't we?" Her voice carried crisp and clean across the distance she kept.

"Exactly," Russ said. "You've got a second chance here, Walter, to do the right thing."

It was true Walter didn't need the house for financial reasons. Roger had left him a rich man. Still, he wanted to dance with the ghosts here, not to sell them.

"We have no intention of interfering with your lifestyle, you know," Russ added, solemn in his effort to reassure. "We'll stay out of your way."

No, they wouldn't, Walter thought, no matter how hard they tried. Death would hit him upside the head again. The glimpses of his former life, which he had come up here to seek out gingerly and then to savor with his breath held, would pop and evaporate as delicate as soap bubbles. The echo of every cha-cha step he could recall would dissolve on contact with any new life Russ and his latest wife began here.

"So what do you say, Sonny?" Russ gave him his dead stare. "Can we proceed with our plan?"

Russ's childhood nickname for him jumped out and rapped Walter on his nose. Yet the belittlement barely registered. He didn't feel he was alone. Roger was here, in spirit. Walter could sense his presence, almost as if his old lover stood behind him. Roger could take Russ down, and he would have the appetite. Walter shut his eyes. There was Roger's face, shaded a bit by that waterfall of silver hair that fell across his forehead. Only now there was relish in his grin and amusement in his eyes, at the prospect of messing with this poor fool, who thought he had the upper hand, by birthright.

"The situation isn't what it seems," Walter said, finally. "Someone wants to buy the house."

Russ was on his feet. "Seriously? You should have said something. Don't toy with us, Walter."

Vivian crossed over to his side, her expression grave with concern.

It stirred Walter to get a rise out of Russ and to see Vivian's face stripped of world-weary amusement. My God, had they signed on with their architect? They must have, to look so stricken.

"Well, I haven't signed a contract," he went on. "He's an old, old colleague of mine. He used to come up here and play music. I was surprised to hear from him too."

It must have been fifteen years since Little Wayne was up here. He came during those first summers after title to the house transferred to Roger, who had the money to buy out Russ and update Granddad's old saltbox just enough to fling it open to great big house parties. Wayne was invited up and alternated on keyboard and horn all night. Walter was right there with him, providing the bassline. The rocky little islets sat close enough to register the buzz and stir, the wag and groove to the tom-tom beat, the rise in tenor as the bodies pulsed. By dawn the music had cooked, until it reduced down to meditation. Guests had either gone home or crashed, but Walter and Wayne remained, witnesses to the scene, sometimes the last men standing, content in the silence of remembered sound.

Those first parties were the ones where the music ran at its purest. Maybe it had frightened Roger a little: to see Walter and Wayne fall under the spell they cast together? Roger had been cautious, possessive of what was his. In any case, each season he had sought out new themes, favored other sounds. There was no snub to Wayne, exactly, but Walter could see how he had neglected his old friend, who faded from his life, and later on departed life altogether, a death that Walter learned of only through the grapevine.

Anyway, it was a pleasure now that Wayne had come forward in memory. First upstairs in the music room and now in the wake of sudden inspiration: Little Wayne, prospective home buyer. If only it were true. Still, it would be yet another pleasure now to channel a message from Wayne's phantom to his brother's ears, to relay to Russ the gist of a conversation he and Little Wayne might have had.

"Funny thing, but his wife wants to live here too," Walter said. "Gail." Wasn't that her name? A singer with a pair of angelic cords. "Wayne told her they could spend the same amount of money and have the key to a pied-à-terre in Paris, with not a care in the world. But he got nowhere with that proposition. This location is the one she wants to plunk her royalties on: a cash deal for a little piece of paradise. 'She wants the piece,' he told me. 'The house, though, I won't lie to you. She'll want to tear it down.'"

Russ stared at Walter for a moment before he spoke. "How can we counter a cash offer? Do I have to remind you that I am your brother?" There was a rare show of emotion in Russ's face, a roiling mix of fear and anger, which turned his skin ashen.

"We wouldn't tear the place down, at least," Vivian jumped in to say. "We would cherish it."

Walter smiled. There was promise in her, he could see, to work around the obstacles that lay in her way. For him, the options were many. He could lend Russ money. He could sell the house and split the proceeds with him. He could offer him and Vivian a site to build elsewhere on the property (No, he would hate that.). Or of course he could simply say yes to their blueprints; yes to their Plan B.

"Give me a moment," he said, and left them there, while he strolled around to the front of the wraparound porch.

There he gazed out across the water at the two rounded rocks, the petite formations, each with a few stray pines, which he and Roger had loved. How would they absorb the new atmosphere, were he to say yes to Russ? The girls weren't impervious to human energy and mood. They would sicken on whatever poison inside Russ had led him to do whatever it was he had done. The wind would blow the toxic fumes all the way from Cameroon.

Like the islets, the house itself seemed to signal a desire to foster fresh life. A jolt of excitement shot through Walter to realize so keenly what it was he had inherited from Roger, his lover; this house Granddad had built. Walter must and could protect it. He was ready now to let Russ and Vivian know his decision. If he had to, he would have had the house taken down to save all that it meant to him. That wouldn't be necessary. He would shower them with money to move on instead.

Walter felt a surge of renewal as he repossessed. Possibilities were opening up. The chamber ensemble should be invited up to write and play new music here. It was the sound of Little Wayne he wanted to hear this evening, however. He would run up and find an old recording or two; up there in one of those cabinets in the music room; let the sound float and settle lightly on top of the years Walter had spent here with Roger. And when Wayne wafted through the house, the sound he made would flow through his fingers and lips with the supple power of water. The little girl isles would respond. Walter knew they would. Their huddled pines would sway and swing. A new note would be sung.

Little Turtle

"So I've given up some of my illusions," Sean said to his mother as they stood on the sidewalk in front of his dorm. "It's in my blood. I'm meant to serve."

Serve? In what way, Sharon wondered. Not in the military, surely. Her son was some kind of Marxist these days.

"I had my epiphany and then my dream of revolution. Now it's more an evolution," he went on. "I can't see fighting in the streets. Ideology isn't the answer, not entirely. We'll need to tinker with another kind of engine to generate the change we need."

That was Sean all over, Sharon thought, the flow always on the bubble. She had never figured out how to wade in and explore all of the possibilities alongside him.

"Well, Dad will be pleased," she said.

"We'll see." Her son sounded distracted, his mind on other things, as usual.

Two years ago, Christmas break, freshman year, the scourge of the world had been unbridled capitalism. Sean had explained why very carefully at the dinner table, but his father wasn't having it.

"Capitalism is a free spirit, not meant to be bridled," Dan had shot back.

Sharon had shaken her head then. For all his success in business, her husband had a thin skin. She took Sean aside, and it took only that one brief exchange to ensure that there would be no more talk of Marx or Piketty in front of his father. Sean understood. He really was a sweetheart that way. He knew how to tend to Dan's sensitivities, especially if they were pointed out to him.

Sharon wasn't particularly concerned about the tack to the left their son had taken. College was the right time to try out outlandish ideas, she figured, before you launched into adulthood, where there was less time and inclination to think beyond the herd. Vaguely she remembered Herbert Marcuse and the Frankfurt School of Critical Theory from a college course she took in the seventies. She hadn't given the philosopher or his school another thought since. For Dan, however, no similar memory could offer reassurance. Dan had not gone to college.

Their son was an outstanding student, and his brilliant academic achievement would bear fruit. She must have said so a hundred times, but it was her brother, Len, who convinced Dan to fret less.

"Your son is no communist," Len had scoffed. "He's smart. That's all. Smart enough to sample the intellectual smorgasbord that a first-rate university offers."

"Then he'll get his fill of Lenin and move on?" Sharon had asked.

"Trotsky's more Sean's speed, I'm sure," Len said, oblivious as always to the sarcasm he provoked in her.

Her brother held a departmental chair and had written several books on cultural semiotics. The fuzzy grasp she and Dan had of the subject only added to Len's awe quotient and Sharon's irritation. Len's reference to a smorgasbord of ideas had at least reassured Dan, she had to concede, so that their household regained the comforting sound of sports talk when Sean was home on break from school. Still, it had been wise, she thought, to run a little interference as the semesters rolled on. The transcripts the school sent home began to reveal their son's higher-level courses in trade unionism in Britain, socialism with Chinese characteristics, the roots of communism that lay in Mozart's *Marriage of Figaro*, and the dialectics to be found in Aunt Jemima. It was best, she felt, to toss the transcript into their home office shredder. Sean's straight A record was all Dan needed to know.

Now, here she stood, outside Sean's dorm, Christmas break, junior year, at his request. He had always taken the train home past semesters. What was going on?

"I quit, Ma."

Since college, he'd taken to calling her Ma instead of Mom, which sounded more workers of the world, she supposed.

"Quit what?"

"College, Ma. I quit school."

"Bummer." The piece of slang, from her own college days, stuck in her throat. Lightheaded, she leaned against the car door, then turned to look at him, as if scrutiny might reveal why she was falling through the center of the earth, as if scrutiny might help her gauge how much farther she would have to drop before she hit bottom. Same as ever from the look of him: tall and dark and slight. That big head of curls. The sharp light in his eyes. His brilliance wasn't obvious, of course. What you did notice right away was his restlessness. He had a long, loose body. His hands were always on the move to help him say what was on his mind. His feet blocked soccer balls like nobody else's. If there was any weakness in him, it was just that Sean was a bit young for his years, a bit naïve. Brilliance could cause a blind spot socially. Still, a stunt like this one was absolutely unlike him.

"But you've always loved school," she said in a burst, "and this school is a great one."

He smiled as if to indulge her. "Trust me. It's not great. Not great at all if you want to learn anything worth knowing."

"What about law school?"

"What about it?"

"It would give you so many opportunities to follow through on your thinking, your ideals."

Her son looked surprised. Then he gave her another pained smile. "The law's a cyanide pill, I'd have to say."

What was that supposed to mean? No, she wouldn't ask. It was too hard to think straight in the rubble of his legal career. The law was where their son was headed. At least that was what she told Dan, perfectly confident in her assumption.

"Let's get out of here," Sean said.

Well, why not? She felt despair creeping in to swamp her initial shock. It wasn't like they were going to get anywhere, here at the curb, surrounded by all his stuff shoved into a few boxes.

Quickly he filled the trunk, jumped into the driver's seat, and they drove out through the campus gates. He was a good driver, alert and confident, better than she was. As they tooled along into the open countryside, black and white cows dotted the landscape. Mother and son whizzed past.

"So what happens now?"

"Oh, I'll find a job."

"Doing what?"

"Fast food, whatever." As usual, Sean's hands flew as he talked, up and down on the steering wheel. "Anything that will get my feet wet and my hands dirty. Get me outside my shelter bubble."

"Oh, God, I can't say I understand," Sharon moaned. She did understand the desire to play with shifting shapes, but shape shifting was something you did in your dreams, or in the studio. You didn't drop out of an Ivy. Not when you were a *wunderkind*.

Years ago, Dan built her a studio on their property with a potter's wheel and a kiln. Later they added a hot shop and a three-furnace setup to blow glass. He also built a wood-working shop for himself. There lay her happiness, in that shared love of craftsmanship, which had drawn her to Dan in the first place. She was proud of the quality of the bedstead, the cabinets, the tables, and chairs he made for their home, quite apart from his success in the design–build business. But then there was the politely disguised lower regard in which a career built on manual skill and labor was held, no matter how lucrative, at least in the bookish world in which they lived.

No one would call Sharon an explorer of ideas but that was what her parents had been, a pair of academics. Sean's mind worked like theirs, and like Len's, too, come to think of it. Even after Sean went off to college and became so ideo-logical, she had found it fun to daydream about his brilliant future. Then slowly but surely would come the indirect bene-fits, the bragging rights that she wished weren't necessary but longed for, because they were, well, for Dan. He was just as good as the next guy who had a string of degrees after his name and a career dotted with international postings. Their son was the proof. Only now Sean was a college dropout? Nothing in such a future made her want to daydream. She felt a terrible loss of imagination.

Along the country road, they passed a sign hung from a pole on a chain, National Register of Historic Places, with an arrow to direct drivers to turn off a few hundred yards ahead.

"Want to check it out?" Sean asked, as if her appetite for such things endured no matter what.

He knew how much she loved old houses: to study the fabrics that covered the chairs, the patterns of paper on the walls, and whether the colors of the paint on the woodwork were true to the period. As a child, Sean never seemed to mind traipsing through some of these old places. Now he must be trying to placate her, which stung, because these days he must see her as a woman of privilege, with luxuries no one deserved: lots of time and space for her own private wonderland, hand-blown.

"No, there's no need to stop," she said.

"Well, I'd like to," he said to her gently, "because this house might help explain what I'm about."

"So you've been here before?"

"Several times," he nodded, "for research. The class hierarchy and strictures are so evident here in what is supposed to be an anomaly on the American scene, built by one of those rags-to-riches Wall Street barons in an earlier Gilded Age. The architecture and the furniture are to die for, though. You'll enjoy them."

They drove in through a set of gates, similar to the ones they had departed through an hour earlier when they left the college. Sean let the car creep along the pebbled drive. A grand home came into sight, which they traveled past to reach a parking lot, with spaces for tour buses and the luck of a lull in the arrival of seniors and schoolchildren.

The ground floor kitchen at the back of the house was empty as they entered from the parking lot. Sharon crossed over to the windows. Outside, a winter moth flitted. On the clapboard of an ancient outbuilding, someone had hung a Christmas wreath. She let its red ribbon entertain her. Watched it whip and whirl. A wunderkind was bound to surprise you, she recognized. If only his decision didn't strike her as so self-destructive. She tried to sympathize with him. Was his decision to quit school a sign that he was cracking under the pressure to meet admittedly high expectations? If so, you'd never know it. Her son's even temperament was intact this morning. To hope he could be persuaded to change his mind and go back to school after semester break wasn't something to count on, given his readiness always to move forward, curious and open to whatever lay ahead. Nonetheless, she and Dan, and certain family members, mentors, and friends would have to put their shoulders into it and give persuasion a try. The effort involved made her want to smoke, although she had quit years ago.

Could there be a positive side to what he was doing? At least Sean would no longer be exposed to so many subversive ideas, which to Dan's mind probably was what the study of liberal arts came down to. Problem was, her husband had kept his faith in academic credentials, with the conviction born of the lack of them. He could see the value in higher education in this day and age, particularly for someone as bright as Sean. Dan had never wavered in his willingness to put their son through school, even after Sean decided to major in history. Besides, Dan was careful with money. Tens of thousands in tuition wasted: that would be his mantra. No, the news would come as a terrible blow.

"Over here," Sean called. "Come and have a look."

She turned away from the window. The kitchen was stark, stripped of the pots and pans and utensils that once gave it life. Her son was pointing to a big framed photograph on the far side of the room. Once she came closer, she could see the rows of men and women that stood to face the camera. They made up the staff that had served in the house more than a century before, according to what was written in spidery ink at the bottom of the sepia print.

"Look at this young woman in the front row, Lorena Casey," Sean said. "Then look at Aurora Betsey, the older, heavy-chested figure in the back row. Ms. Betsey's face is resolved. Lorena Casey's, on the other hand, is still open to possibility. What's in that crooked smile of hers? I see a mix of fear and hope. She climbs those steep stairs with the heavy soup tureen in a new country, one that brags about its equality, one where she might rise above the ground floor someday. Is there a better future here for her in America or not? She's not sure yet. Or so I like to imagine," her son added with a rueful smile. He turned to look at his mother inquiringly, his large dark eyes quite serious, and hopeful, too, apparently, that the photograph might speak to her the way it spoke to him.

Sharon nodded her head slightly. This kind of imagining was something she used to encourage in Sean when he was little. What was the point of a visit to a historical site, she used to say to him, if not to try and feel what it must have been like to live there in the past? Now it was painful to see that hopeful look in his eyes, because she wasn't able to share his excitement. She couldn't cotton to the lives of Lorena Casey or Aurora Betsey, not the way she could to the lives of the people who once owned and roamed the rooms upstairs; it was the qualities of their possessions that captivated her. No, she couldn't fathom her own son as he spouted talk that must have come straight out of his seminars.

"A hundred years ago, the daily lives of Lorena and the rest of the kitchen staff here were filled with dumb repetition, aching labor, with little to show for it: And that's still the case in so many places in this country. My objective now is to walk their walk. You know, get 'nickel and dimed,' but also to learn where their dreams lie." Excited, Sean's voice picked up speed. "Don't get me wrong. It's a great thing, actually: a privilege for me to try to become as real as they are. That's where nobility lies, you know, in the endurance of tedium."

"Really? That sounds over the top, Sean, at least to me."

Now that he had removed his ski parka, she saw what a shadow he had become, all skin and bones. His shrunken body was alarming, a sign of his mania, it seemed to his mother. Brilliance had its downside.

"Simone Weil understood. She chose to work on the

factory floor."

"Simone Weil? I thought she was a Jewish mystic."

"She was a lot of things." Sean waved away the point, clearly a distraction from what he wanted to say. "She was frail, actually pretty clumsy, but what mattered was she was kin to her fellow laborers; she was right there alongside them, sharing in the hardness of their lives."

"Okay, but you can make money and still be a good person, right? Ambition and success aren't disqualifying, are they? I mean, Dad, for instance, worked his way up honestly."

"Of course," Sean said, offhandedly. "Dad is great. But I don't need to prove myself the same way he did, Ma, and I don't need to live in a protective bubble."

Sharon let her chin fall to meet the scarf at her neck. Sean was still quite young when she quietly gave him to understand that his father could be socially awkward sometimes and hypersensitive to snobbery and rebuffs, which weren't necessarily there. Sean was quick to learn how to distract Dan and lighten him up. It was a knack she had counted on, been grateful for, which was why his academic choices had been troubling, because they troubled Dan. So it hurt to hear Sean describe his father's limitations with such offhand detachment. She was reminded of something Len once said to her when Sean was still in high school. She had tentatively floated the idea that their son might like to join his father in business, given what a success Dan had made of it.

"Why would Sean want to walk in his father's footsteps,

just to move past them," Len had said. She was used to an older brother who was quick to dismiss any idea of hers. What had wounded her was how quick he was to dismiss her husband. "Dan's aims in life are too ordinary for someone as gifted as Sean."

"So Lorena Casey reminds me of Annie Collins," Sean was saying. "Annie came along a generation or so later than Lorena, of course, but to be in service in a house like this one wouldn't have been that different in the 1920s."

"Who's Annie Collins?"

"She's in one of those photographs at home," he said, "in the upstairs hall."

When they moved into the house fifteen years ago, Sharon and Dan had hung that whole corridor with photographs. From albums inherited from both sets of parents, they selected the shots that came closest to art. At first they were décor. Now they were just a blur, or at least they were to Sharon.

"She was the one I called 'Moonie.' Because you told me she was 'moonfaced.' Remember?"

"Well, I can't say that I do, but, yes, you liked to ask questions and stomp and shout along that hallway when you were a little guy."

"I used to love to stare at those faces. I still do. What I notice about Annie, now, though, is not the shape of her face but her smile. Wouldn't it be great if Lorena Casey's crooked smile had grown into one as cool as Annie's? Like the cat that ate the canary."

"How do you know her name?"

"Annie Collins was a cousin of Dad's father. It's no wonder you don't know. We've seen so little of the Dean side of the family."

Sharon had never been comfortable with the roughhouse Deans. They had mimicked the way Sharon talked, the few times she was set down in their midst. They seemed to think she was as much of an ornament as the ones she made.

"Dad and I spent a little time talking about his family last year," Sean went on. "I was curious to hear what he could tell me. Annie's name was mentioned in passing. It turns out my grandfather was a streetcar conductor; my grandmother was a laundress. Well, of course, I was psyched, Ma. I had to egg Dad on."

"What do you mean?"

"To appreciate his family, his ancestry, to be proud of his background. So then he did get interested in tracing his genealogy."

"He did? I didn't know that." It disturbed her a little to hear that they might share a world apart from her. "You and Dad are closer than I realized."

"Maybe we are." Sean said. He looked at her calmly, as if there was nothing very surprising about the possibility. "It was a good conversation," he said, "but we get along fine without a lot of talk."

"Let's go home now," she said, worn out by his boundless intensity.

"Don't you want to see the furniture first? It's all real, all good."

"Please don't try to butter me up, Sean. I'm ready now, except for a trip to the restroom."

"That's not what I'm trying to do," he said, sounding surprised. "I respect your eye for beauty a lot."

In the bathroom stall, she made a call to Dan on her cell. "We're running late. Sean wanted to stop at a historic house to show me an old photo: of the kitchen staff, actually; one of the maids. He's connected the dots to a photo we have in our hall upstairs. Someone on your side named Annie Collins."

"I know which one she is. Sean asked me about her once."

"And here I thought all you guys did was talk about ball games."

Dan couldn't remember what they had said exactly, but he did remember that it had felt good to be standing there with Sean, who seemed to take a real interest in his side of the family, there in front of the photo of Annie Collins and a few other relatives in the hallway upstairs.

The stress in his wife's voice brought him back to the moment.

"He's pretty charged up," she was saying. "I think he really needs a break."

"Well, it's Christmas. He'll get a break. So why didn't he

take the train home? Is there a problem?"

Sharon sighed. "It's a long story, and I'm exhausted. We're headed to the car now. I just want to get home."

"Okay, baby. Come on home."

After Sharon clicked off, Dan put the Cowboys versus Patriots on mute and began a slow circuit of the room, furnished with its mix of venerable old cabinets from her late parents and the silver maple table and chairs he had made himself. Shards of glass in some of Sharon's best pieces gleamed on the mantelpiece.

In a less preoccupied moment, he might have been aware of his surroundings, of the love he and his wife shared of certain things well-made by hand and nature. Growing up, he had learned to shield the softer side of himself. To value anything of beauty, especially something rare or fragile, gentle or subtle, was sneered at by his older sisters, who taught him to take life by the short hairs. He saw the value in their approach, too, just not in the all-purpose way they did.

Sharon had not sounded good on the phone. As usual, she's probably trying to shield me from something she thinks will bug me, he thought, a big old ruddy guy like me. He had always been her head case. "I worry about you," she would say, and he had learned to pick up on the cues that signaled one of her bursts of concern. A shadow would cross her face, or her voice would rise in the tinkling way it could in social situations, sure signs that she was going to sail in and try to save him from an awkward moment. "Your little complex is showing again." How many times had he heard her say that? Sharon had never actually said that, not in so many words, kind soul that she was, but he was able to follow her thoughts about as well as the game on TV without the sound. Well, he didn't blame her. His lack of social graces was pretty ingrained. Still, her concern was less warranted than it used to be. In middle age, he had grown more comfortable with himself, as-is. Sharon hadn't seemed to notice, or else the early hope a young wife had to perfect her husband might spring eternal, he supposed.

Thirty years ago, when his business was beginning to take off, he saw the need to take some accounting courses at the community college. He found them useful in more ways than one. It was through the door to one of the studio arts classrooms that he first spotted Sharon. Fresh out of the Rhode Island School of Design, she had taken a job as a ceramics teacher, her strawberry blonde hair falling forward as she showed her students how to work their hands into deep, red clay. Rose of Sharon, as it turned out. Her mom, the biblical scholar, chose to christen her only child with the name and could give you chapter and verse. Dan had taken in stride Sharon's earnest, erudite mother, as well as her harried and distracted father, who ran a research team at one of the university cancer centers in Boston. They had been good-natured people, easy to like.

For their part, they admired Dan, Sharon told him at one point. His being ten years older went unmentioned, whereas his integrity was noted with approval. They must have also noted his rapid success as a local builder. When the time came, they accepted the marriage wholeheartedly. Somehow it was just assumed that Dan would embrace their milieu, a new word in his life, once he adjusted to his social step up, which they were all too tactful to notice.

Some things were easy to get used to, like the swimming pool and the chef-grade kitchen, and the putting green, because they were things acquired through his own success. Other niceties and the subtleties of the upper middle class were beyond him. When Sean was a toddler, Sharon told Dan she wanted to move to another neighborhood, because of the good schools, but there was nothing wrong with the ones where they were. What she really wanted was to return to where she had always felt comfortable, which was not in a neighborhood where self-made entrepreneurs settled into mega mansions. So they had moved here to raise their son in a neighborhood similar to the one in which she was raised, among the kind of people with skills and accomplishments so different from his: neurosurgery, for example, and the translation into English of Japanese novels and poetry, which impressed him but also left him at a loss. Yet, after fifteen years here, what he used to find intimidating bothered him far less than it used to. It was okay to stand apart a little from the crowd. Because who would he be if he weren't who he always had been, even if he was largely self-made?

On the big colored screen, the players tackled and tumbled, up and down the field, while Dan padded around in his slippers. He loved Sharon and trusted that she still

loved him. He loved his business. Those were the fortunate givens of his life. Nothing and nobody, however, had
ever reached in and grabbed hold of him like Sean, so that
something inside Dan rose up and carried him, made him
buoyant. What amazed Dan was the way Sean took life head
on. Born that way. All he and Sharon had ever had to do
was stand back and watch him go. What other people called
child-raising barely registered on their screen. When Sean
got into a top university, Dan couldn't have been prouder.
Only something had gone wrong. Sean had arrived at an elite
institution, ready to go places, and then he got himself stuck
in the muck of other people's hard-bitten lives, this mania
for the common man. What was that about?

"He's romanticized the working class" was Sharon's way
of putting it, which made Dan uneasy. Did she think he and
his side of the family were to blame for their son's flight of
fancy? They might be working class, but none of them was
a Marxist. It had been wrenching to see his son spring feet
first into some kind of serious socialism. It made it harder
to continue to trust in higher education. Yet he did see that
Sean really loved books and to chase big ideas.

Annie Collins. Sharon had mentioned her as if she offered
some clue, some way to understand their son's thinking. He
would go up and take a fresh look at this woman he had met
only once when he was a boy. After a Sunday dinner with
extended family, it was his young parents who were asked
to see their cousin home, to drive her out into the countryside, thirty or forty miles from Cleveland, to a manor house,

which belonged to one of those industrialists who made a fortune on the Great Lakes. Annie had found work there as a maid when she left Ireland as a teenager in the early 1920s. By the time his father took her photo, Annie was a woman in her fifties, who had served nearly thirty years in the household, whose magnificent wrought-iron gate she stood beside as they said goodbye.

With its high contrasts, his dad's photograph was striking, which was why he and Sharon had hung it upstairs. For the woman pictured, however, Dan felt nothing in particular. It was his parents muttering after they had dropped her off and were driving home that was caught in memory. Sleepily, he had listened from the back seat in the dark: first his mother's voice, with its note of discovery: "Oh, she's quite the happy snob," and then his father's grunt of assent: "she thinks she's a member of that big shot's family."

A little harsh, his parents were, he had come to feel. Annie had been a farmer's daughter who had arrived in search of a husband she never found. What chance would she have had to rise into the middle class? She had no children to dream for, either. Like servants the world over, she settled for status by association. It was unkind to mock her for "delusions of grandeur," the way Mom had, but she and Dad were second-generation Americans, successful enough to have grown impatient. He understood that they would have liked it better if Annie had worked almost anywhere else, had done anything but collaborate with the great wealth she served. His parents' opinion hardly mattered, if the photo was any clue. Annie's face was strong, surprisingly confident. Pride shone there, triumph even: as if she did own all that lay behind the massive gate, left open just enough for Dad's camera to catch a glimpse into the garden. Yes, delusions of grandeur must be satisfying, if you could pull them off, Dan thought, the way Annie seemed to have done, from her sense of possession, right down to the small pleasure of tweaking her relatives, who worked as streetcar conductors and the like.

What would Sean make of her, this happy snob? Dan had said little about her when he and Sean had stood here months ago. He had much preferred to bask in his son's enthusiasm about people with backgrounds like his own, even if it was enthusiasm of the cornball kind, which would have made his sisters' eyes roll, and his own to roll, too, inwardly. What if he told his son now that Annie had sucked up to her titan employer, that his own sisters would have mocked Sean's praise of the working class to kingdom come? Would it burst his son's bubble? Dan doubted it. His son was no shallow thinker. He would find some way to run with the new information, the way a player on the field ran with the ball.

No, to unmask Annie as a snob didn't tempt him. It would just be scoring points. Dan wanted to avoid arguments about politics with Sean. The ones at Christmas, freshman year, had come close to breaking skin. Much as he continued to hope that the cloud of his son's unwelcome world view would pass, Dan thought he had learned to take things as they came; to play out to the finish line, the way he did in business, once he had done all he could to shape the outcome. Back downstairs, he turned up the sound on the TV. The quarterback for the Patriots made it to the forty-two yard line, and the optimism that coursed through Dan extended to his son and to his thoughts about his future. For sure, the shape of his life would take time to gel. Whatever Sean's life was going to be, by God, let it be his own.

When Sharon came out of the rest room, Sean stood waiting. "I called Dad," she told him. "So he wouldn't worry."

"So you told him I dropped out?"

She sucked in some air and let it out again. "I meant to. Then I decided not to."

"Well, good," he nodded. "You know, it was great of you to pick me up today. I thought it was best to break the news to you first. I was even hoping you would understand why I'm dropping out, but, hey, I get that it's hard to understand other people."

She heard the disappointment in his voice, compliments of a mother's power. Too bad she wasn't wielding much of it in the ways that mattered at the moment.

The parking lot was busier than when they had arrived. Several school buses were pulling into the lot. As they reached the Subaru, it struck Sharon what to do.

"Drop me at the train station," she said. "You take the car. It's got all your stuff. Do your field work. See how things go."

"Field work?" he hooted. "I'm not a researcher, Ma. I just

want to get in touch with how people work in this country now, people with my roots."

"Dad's roots," she corrected him. "Look," she said, "I don't want you to come home, just to drop your bomb, at Christmas time. If this is what you want to do, then get on with it. Follow through on your ideas. Find a gig somewhere. Try your luck. After that, you can tell Dad what's up. He'll suffer less if you have something going on by the time you tell him."

"But I don't like hiding the news from him. I'm not looking for an easy way out. I can face the consequences."

"We're facing the consequences right now, my friend," Sharon snapped. "We've heard a lot about what you want today. How about us? Don't you think you owe us some consideration?"

"Of course I do," he pleaded. "This isn't some adolescent rebellion. It's because I've learned enough to know what I need to do in the world. And maybe I will go back to school someday. Who knows? Not on Dad's dime, of course. Right now he deserves to hear from me face to face."

"No, it's the last thing he deserves. Your quitting will hit him hard, and you know it."

"Dad doesn't need to be kid-gloved on my account. He can handle it."

"How can you say that?" Sharon was exasperated. "You know that's not true." Her voice rang out across the parking lot.

"The hell I do," Sean shouted, which shocked her. He was always such a sweetheart, never disrespectful.

Two preteen girls from one of the school buses looked their way, interest aroused in their round blue eyes. Sharon got into the passenger seat and lowered her voice. "C'mon, Sean. Hop in. You know it's a good idea. Take your break before you decide."

"What do you plan to tell him?" Sean got into the car but didn't turn the key in the ignition. He sat there, looking glum, waiting to hear what his mother had to say.

Sharon sat there, too, waiting to see what might come to mind. Well, she could tell Dan that Sean had decided to use his semester break to do a field study in one of those ghost factory towns, not far from his university. The interviews had to be done at Christmas time to get a sense of how holiday customs and attitudes had changed in a down-and-out economy. The opportunity was a last-minute one from his department head. He was sorry to miss spending Christmas with them, but this quest to understand working class America was his passion; it was part of his heritage. He had asked her to come up, because he wanted to walk her through the decision, so she might understand it, rather than just blurt it out on the phone. Sure, the Subaru was going to be a big help, but he hadn't asked for it. The bus would have been fine. She had urged him to take the car.

Whether Dan would accept this story was questionable. Sharon's only real hope was that he would at least pretend to, because the alternative would be less tempting to accept, namely that they had a crazy, mixed-up kid on their hands, who didn't know what he was doing. Even if Dan doubted the story, he might sense the need to buy some time, too.

"You're creative, Ma. You always come up with something."

It was a flip remark by which Sean regained his cool. He turned the key in the ignition, and they drove back through the fields of black and white cows. She could feel his mood had plunged; the excited state he had been in all morning had vanished.

"My mind's made up, Mom," he said after a while. He spoke quietly, wearily. "But you're right. It is Christmas. I can wait a little bit to tell him. I'll find a job and, while I won't lie to him, I guess it's fair to say I'm doing research."

"Aren't we all?" Sharon giggled. Relief elated her. "Say, you're calling me Mom again."

Sean nodded but offered no explanation for the shift in the way he addressed her. Was it a parting gift? Anyway, she liked it. At the train station, she turned to give him a peck on the cheek and to murmur, "You're doing us a service, Sean, even if it doesn't seem that way."

"You take such good care of Dad," he said, as if there were something remarkable about it.

"I've tried," she sighed. "But I wonder sometimes how much I've succeeded."

"You're doing fine, Mom," he said, his gentleness returning. "You shouldn't worry too much. Dad's much stronger than you realize."

"What makes you think so?"

"I think he's come to like the life you've created. He can see through your eye of beauty pretty well."

It ruffled her, what he said. Because he didn't know everything, did he, especially not about beauty and what it was made of.

"Well, I've always counted on you to help me," she found herself saying, looking him straight in the eye. "You know. To help protect the bubble you now want to escape."

She squeezed his hand, and was quick to exit the car, but then she couldn't resist her desire to turn back to look at him.

He was crying.

Startled, she rushed back across the street to him, but the Subaru shot forward, and he was gone.

She hadn't seen Sean cry since he was a small boy, which took her back to those early days when he was just starting to go to school. "C'mon, little turtle," she egged him on, Dr. Seuss style, when he brought home his first report card and failed to get straight As. In no time at all, he learned to excel and win on his own. To see the tears on his face just now, though, she had to wonder. Could it be they had come full circle, she and her little turtle, and he was back at the starting gate again?

Still. Sean had driven off with a plan, which did stir some

hope in her, the way forward motion usually did. Other possibilities lay out there beyond jurisprudence. Sean might become a great ethnologist, or even a brilliant economist, one who had something to say about alternative monetary systems, based on an early affection for socialism, as well as a later disavowal, which in turn would lead to prestigious public service. Yes, it was a new way to imagine their son's future, one to perfect on the train home, so that, by the time Dan met her at the station, she would be filled with good cheer to spare.

The Pool Inside
the Villa

As the plane reached cruising altitude, Christine let her mind drift. She had been to San Juan once before. Certain images from that long-ago trip arose even before the flight attendant could hand her a bottle of water. There was that hippie sundress she had packed, so thin and cheap. Yet it was fancy compared with the threadbare jeans she usually wore, same as Geoff, back in the day. When Elena had caught sight of the dress, she just shook her head at how bad it would look under the chandeliers of the casino. Too small to lend something of her own, she had another solution, not to worry, and led the way up the spiral staircase to the villa's master bedroom, where heavy drapes shut out the heat and light. A pair of cufflinks and a silver-handled brush lay on a dresser, vulnerable in the absence of their owners. They lay there still, in Christine's mind, more than twenty years later. So did the intricate coverlet on the bed. It would be some time before she began to focus on embroidery, with its remarkable stability, the basic stitches used to patch and mend cloth the world over. Textiles were her business now. They also were her passion, careful though she was to maintain a certain reserve with clients, careful to let each piece of fabric speak for itself.

Elena had opened one of several closets, and together they fingered their way through the contents. The dress they chose was dark blue silk, very simple. Today Christine would have found it humiliating to rifle through someone else's things. At the time all that seemed to matter was the feel of the silk against her skin, and the way it clung to her body, just right.

They had all been friends at the University of Michigan. Right after graduation, Elena had talked Karl into giving her home island a try. Nobody but Geoff was finding it easy to put together an adult life. Still, Karl had taken on a special challenge, to stake his future in another culture. Maybe he was feeling lonely when he invited college friends to share in the luxury of the villa that he and Elena were house sitting for his boss, a Citibank executive not much older than he was. Maybe Karl had wanted to show off a little, too. The villa in Old San Juan had awakened Christine to what money could mean at a time when it seemed they would never have much. She and Geoff had to blow their paychecks to fly down. He didn't care about the finer things in life, except to capture them in the best light and at the right angle with his cameras. She admired his lack of desire but was beginning to see that she didn't share it.

At the core of the villa lay the pool, set into an interior courtyard, open to the sky and to the play of light. By noon the water was a thrilling turquoise, deepening into the blue hour of evening when the fronds of tropical plants cast shadows on the adobe walls. Karl's boss had given him access to the premium liquor in the patio bar. Those bottles, their very shape and color, had beckoned to Christine in particular. Their wicked beauty winked at her even now.

Each morning of their stay, Geoff had joined her out on the patio, where she lay stretched out on one of the chaises, to recover from her spree the night before. The possibility that the two of them could linger alone by the pool was tantalizing, because by midmorning Elena would already be off at her hole-in-the-wall storefront, trying to hang her first collection of local art. Karl had his job at the bank, and Tom, another old friend from Ann Arbor days, would be playing the casino's slot machines.

Only Gert had interfered. She would come out to the kitchen, open to the patio, and sit straight across from them in their lounge chairs. She pulled out her sketchbook, often furiously, because Tom's gambling upset her, and so they bore her misery. As she drew, she heckled in that German-tinged voice of hers.

"You're so wasted, Chrissie. What's your purpose in life?"

At the time Christine still thought there might be a big bang answer that eluded her as she lay there in the hot sun with a tee-shirt over her face and grimaced. Only Gert would ask such a question. How high-minded she was for such a campy dresser.

"What a cockatoo," Elena had said of Gert when she first set eyes on her. No wonder. Coming out of the master bedroom with the borrowed blue dress, Elena and Christine had paused at the top of the spiral staircase before making their descent, which was tricky. So was the handrail, covered with decorative wrought-iron leaves to look like a tree branch. Through the balusters, they could look straight down into the foyer. There sat Gert in the rope swing, suspended above the shallow ornamental pool. A tiara, tufted with feathers, sat in her short, yellow hair. At her neck an IUD hung among the silver chains as if it were costume jewelry. Six feet tall, with a big frame, she was trim and supple enough to look good in her bikini.

She wouldn't have been perched there at all, of course, if not for sheer chance. Christine had introduced her to Tom when the three of them crossed paths at a restaurant in Manhattan. He had never taken anything seriously as far as Christine knew, especially women. Yet he sounded serious when he confided that Gert was "amazingly real," unlike "people in patent law, where I've ended up." Instantly, they were a couple, and Tom brought her down to the villa.

Elena had given Christine a sidewise glance on the staircase. "I'm surprised she's a friend of yours."

"From high school," Christine muttered.

She was the one who had pressed for the friendship.

What did she have in common with a girl whose parents were a couple of burned-out artists from the wrong side of the Berlin Wall? Christine had been damaged teenage goods, she would have to say of herself, seeking refuge not from communism but from sadness, confusion, a shy sense of social alienation. Who better to hide behind than Gert with her sheer size and flamboyance? And once Gert saw how faint the welcome was going to be for a big foreign girl, who dressed like a peacock but said owlish things, she no longer rebuffed Christine.

I was the lucky one, Christine thought. Gert showed her how everyday life ran deeper, freer, mellowed by reflection if convention was cast aside. Her mom painted six-foot oils in the living room, while her dad played prepared piano, to get the tonal effects of objects set between the strings, like an East German John Cage. To think you could create your own life was news to Christine. She was excited, if unsure how to go about it. Then the two girls went off to different colleges at a time when no social media existed to make them constantly aware of each other's every move. When Christine returned to New York, Gert was no longer her guide. Geoff was the artist in her life by then.

Christine never did get to linger by the villa pool. Once she could face the noontime sun, Geoff wanted to head out into the streets of the old city. While she idled on the cobblestones with a headache, he took pictures. His success as a photographer was just emerging, and his freewheeling style jibed with the headiness of realizing his talent. Meanwhile, what a joke she had been, an entry-level city planner, calculating how to move from Point A to Point Z, when she was still so prone to losing her footing at night, flaming out somewhere in the kaleidoscopic downtown art scene, while Geoff breezed along, lighter on his feet than she was, buoyed by his search for another perfect image.

It was near sunset when everyone had gathered to drink rum punch as prelude to the last night of their stay. A cocktail table was set up in the foyer, and the ornamental pool was backlit for glamour. The plan was to go to dinner and then on to the casino to play blackjack in the grand salon. Christine circled down the difficult stairs in the stiletto heels, which Elena had snagged from the master bedroom to match the borrowed dress. Gert watched her every step.

"So you are joining us this evening?" Christine asked as she touched down. "I thought you hated casinos."

"That's a given, Chrissy, but I want to be with Tom tonight, even it means being gawked at on the streets."

Gert would turn heads, it was true, towering in her glittering clothes. Even in her borrowed heels, Christine had to gaze up into her old friend's sharp eyes, shadowed blue with makeup. "Well, you do look good," she said.

"Well, you've looked better. The color isn't right on you, and you're wrong to borrow that dress."

Christine ignored her and headed toward the rum punch,

not wanting to start happy hour with an argument. Elena had invited a few people, whom she and Karl had been getting to know: a local trade attorney and a couple of academics on sabbatical from Toronto, who took an interest in Puerto Rican art and Elena's efforts to showcase it. Oh, how doctrinaire they had seemed at the time, those Canadians, their names long lost to her, harping on American hegemony. The evening had started cordially, but even the pleasantries had a sharp edge.

"How's your gallery coming?" the attorney asked Elena.

"It's been a bitch," she laughed, and mentioned that Karl had just called. He had to work late.

The lawyer had nodded and said it was wise to do well at Citi. "He won't be resented there for poaching on slim pickins' the way he might be elsewhere on the island."

The Canadians weighed in then.

"Slim pickins'. How do you say that in Spanish?" the shorter one asked.

The tall one sighed. "Karl's a nice guy, but he's got blood on his hands, whether he knows it or not."

"Well, I won't hold it against him," the attorney spoke again. "He's not arrogant, even if his government is, not to mention his employer."

"Whoa, there," Tom chimed in. "We're fellow Americans, aren't we?" He had swept into the living room on his way to the pool. He hadn't dressed for dinner yet and was ready for a swim, his terrycloth robe tied loosely over his speedo.

The lawyer shrugged. "We don't get much of a say in things, though, do we."

Right enough," the short Canadian said. "How would you like it, Tom? A bloody empire parked on your doorstep, and you have to take a back seat."

"I wouldn't worry too much," Tom said. "America will go the way of all empires."

"Meaning what," the short Canadian demanded.

"The empire will fade," Tom answered him.

The attorney smiled. "Sounds like a Hollywood movie."

"Do you really think American power will recede?" the tall Canadian asked. He sounded in earnest.

"Sure I do," Tom said. "It's the natural course of things. What goes up must come down."

The Canadian's face fell. "Oh," he said. "A cliché."

Tom stepped in close and gave his shoulder a squeeze. "At least we hombres all like to party, right?"

The man shrank away, while his shorter colleague got in another smart remark. "And when your party's over, the rest of us can clean up the mess."

"Yeah, probably," Tom said and let out a laugh. Christine could still hear his embarrassment but also a young delight.

Snark and rum, poured with a heavy hand, had made for a toxic brew. She had fled the cocktail hour in search of fresh air. Out on the patio, the sky was nearing the end of its blue hour, when the light had a special quality, which flattered blondes, Geoff once told her early on, when he had taken many pictures of her, and playfully she had asked him if she needed to be twilit to look good. She was part of his art, she liked to think. Except the light itself was his true love and the true source of the beauty of his photographs. These were things she was just then beginning to allow herself to know.

She took off the stiletto heels and began to pad around the perimeter of the pool. Only she slipped and lost her footing. For a split second, her body arced into the air before she fell back into the water. The Citibank dress ballooned around her. Then it clung like a second skin as she surged to the surface. The rum had left her woozy. The water awoke her. She lay back and stared up at the sky, floating quietly, breathing deeply, until the shock began to ease and dissolve. Once she regained calm, she made her way over to the far corner of the pool. There she treaded water lightly, at a distance from the main stretch of the patio, able to see anyone who might have heard the splash.

Elena came out and spotted her first. "Oh, my God, Tina," she laughed. "Tsk, tsk."

Geoff slid into view behind her. "Ahoy out there! Enjoying yourself?" His voice was relaxed and reassuring.

Christine had stared at the water. "Yes, I love the moonlight on the skin of chlorine," she called back to him. It felt fabulous to be dissolving into blackening ink.

He came down to the deep end, then, crouching to hand her a gin and tonic. She had been grateful to put the glass to her lips, with its clean whiff of juniper to chase away the memory of the rum punch, which had been sweet and heavy in her mouth. She tilted her glass to drink the last drops. *Subo al cielo.* The guitarist had sung just the right words the other afternoon as they walked the streets in the baking heat. To ascend into heaven was what Christine wanted to do, too, as she hovered there in the pool. Yes, she knew what went up must come down. That was okay. She would just have to suffer through another hangover in the morning.

Tom strode out and flung his robe over a chair. There was a loud crack as he dove into the pool. Gert came out after him, drawn by the sound, apparently. Then she did something she hadn't done before. She crossed the invisible demarcation she had imposed and stood poolside, if at a safe distance from the edge.

"Tom!" she called. "C'mon, get out, it's time to go."

He swam laps with precision and speed. Only Gert could assume he would heed her command. At the shallow end, he stopped long enough to say, "I'll be out in a jiffy and then we'll go."

"What about our dinner reservations?"

"No problem. We'll get there."

Christine had felt sudden pity for her old friend, who had frozen stock still on the terracotta apron. Everyone knew Gert avoided the pool. Nobody but Christine, however, knew just how much Gert feared the water. Why was she afraid? She couldn't or wouldn't say. How much courage it must have taken, Christine thought, to come and stand so close to the pool and all because she had fallen in love with an avid swimmer. Clearly she had been challenging herself already. For Gert to sit in the basket swing above the ornamental pool, Christine knew, had been a feat even though it contained but a few inches of water. With the aquarium on the kitchen counter, Gert had met success. She loved to draw the Clown and Angel fish that swam there.

"Go sit in the kitchen, Gert," Christine called, but Gert paid no attention.

The trade attorney came out. In the dark, he bumped against Gert, sending her stumbling to the very edge of the pool. She let out a scream. His hand shot out to steady her.

"Don't touch me," she hissed.

Startled, he let go of her arm. He spotted Elena and headed toward her.

"Hey," Gert yelled after him.

He turned around.

"Not you," she said to him. "Elena."

"What's the matter," Elena said, cool and flat.

"Can you give me a hand?" Gert had wrapped her arms around herself. Her voice sounded as young as a child's.

"Go ahead and help her," the attorney said. "I can fix my own drink."

"She's a pain." Elena shifted to Spanish. "I can't wait until she goes home."

"Even so," he answered without emotion.

"Give her a minute. She'll get it together," Elena muttered and led her guest over to the lounge chairs. By then their Spanish ran too fast for Christine to follow. They had been attractive to watch. Elena's dark hair cascaded down her bare shoulders onto her white sheathe. The attorney had a sharp, intelligent face.

Gert cried out again. Her voice had gone high and slippery, close to panic. In her fright she had turned pigeon-toed in her impossibly tall designer shoes.

Exasperated, Elena put her hands on her hips and scoffed. "What's the problem? Did you see a mouse? Did a little rodent run over your Jimmy Choo shoes?" She laid on a heavy accent.

The "choo-choos" made Christine chuckle and caused Elena to round on her.

"What about you, Christine? How about you help your good friend?"

The gin had made Christine sloppy. Still, she made an effort to splash her way over to the ladder. "Hang on," she called. "I'm coming."

"No, don't get out, Chrissy," Gert shouted. "I need you, Elena. *Por favor*," she had pleaded.

"*Basta*," Elena barked. "Such theatrics." The harshness of the Spanish word seemed to have its desired effect. At last

Gert seemed to give up. Her big body slumped, and her head hung down. She began to cry. She covered her face with her hands and shook with tears.

Elena watched, clearly intrigued. Then she went into the kitchen and came out with a dishcloth. "Here, let's put this over your head, and you won't see anything to scare you."

On tiptoe she reached up and placed the cloth on Gert's head and let it drop down to cover her face. The sight was unforgettable: a big woman dressed in fishnet stockings and twinkly rhinestones stood before them in an odd form of purdah. In a few moments, they could see Gert's body relax. She seemed calmer. The dishcloth seemed to be working as something of a sedative.

Until Elena exploded into laughter. "Big bird," she shouted. "You remind me of Big Bird."

Gert began to cry again, this time without reservation, as steady as rain, abandoned sounding, which truly seemed to impress Elena.

"Please, Elena," the attorney said. "Give it a rest. She won't take my hand. So please give her yours."

"I just can't believe you," Elena said, as she took hold of Gert's hand, and her gleeful face did shine with a kind of innocence, her honest disbelief.

At last Tom came to the end of his laps. He climbed out of the pool, put his arm around Gert, and gave her a squeeze as he nudged Elena away. "Here, let's take this thing off," he said, and made a pass at the dishcloth. "Leave it!" Gert screeched, and he jumped back, unsure of himself, it seemed.

The taller Canadian came out in time to witness the scene. "That's no way to treat an aqua phobic," he told Tom. "Help her move away from the pool. Gently now. Gently."

"Watch what you call my girlfriend," Tom retorted. "She's way too cool for a label like that." As usual, he spoke more in jest than annoyance.

Geoff sidled up then, the ablest Gert whisperer among them that night. "Don't worry," he said, with that light cheerfulness of his. "You're safe with us. Okay if we go in now?" She let him take her hand, while Tom took the other. Ever so gently, the two men led her inside.

Watching them go, Elena shook her head as if to signal her lasting disbelief. "Vámanos," she said to her attorney friend. "Karl is waiting for us." On the way into the house, she glanced back at the pool. "Are you coming, Christine? You better hurry if you are."

"No. Tell Geoff to go without me," Christine said. She shut her eyes to await the tranquility that would arrive after everyone was gone. What a stressful evening it had been. She was the ringmaster, though, wasn't she, leading the circus parade out here in the first place by falling into the pool? It was hard to believe the evening would have gone well anyway. Yet for a long time, she would carry the shame of the spectacle, because it felt like somebody should.

"Are you okay?"

The sharp voice at her ear caused her eyes to flutter.

Christine looked up at a man, who was squatting to peer down at her. It took her a moment to recognize the shorter of the two Canadians. "Yes, I'm fine," she muttered. "Don't worry about me."

"Oh, but I do," the Canadian said. "You're drunk, dear."

No she wasn't, or at least not nearly as much as she might have been.

"You've got no business being in a pool."

She looked up into his face. All judgment, no pity. Yet he offered her his outstretched hand. She grabbed hold of his palm, fat and pink, strong enough to pull her out. The water fell away from her body. Her skin had turned slightly blue, to match the dress that clung to the lithe curves of her twenty-some years.

The man was quick to let go of her hand.

"So it must be great to be Canadian," it occurred to her to say.

"No need to get carried away."

"Seriously," she said. "I might even like to move to Toronto."

The man grunted. "Whatever for?"

"Because I've been thinking about what you said about America," she heard herself saying.

"Oh, that," the little man said and swatted the air. "Cocktail chatter."

"No, you were serious." Christine challenged him.

"Abuse of power was what I meant to criticize," he answered her. "A problem every great nation has faced."

"Well, I'm sick of us!" Christine's voice rose high and shrill, in frustration. She didn't have the goods to explain what drove the disgust she felt. "We need to grow up," was all she could think to shout. Then her anger collapsed, leaving her exhausted, the damp dress sticky against her skin.

The Canadian didn't seem surprised at all by her outburst. He just spoke to her, soft and slow. "It's best to start at home, they say, when you're cleaning up your act."

"Oh, I intend to start at home," she said, nodding several times in agreement, but the Canadian was already moving away, as if in a hurry, toward the house.

"Adiós, adolescence," she called out to him and his retreating khaki sports jacket.

"Olé!" he shouted back. "And good luck," he added over his shoulder, before disappearing from view, headed out toward the larger world he must prefer.

It was late morning by the time Christine woke with no recollection of how she had come to lie in bed. Slowly she wound her way down the spiral stairs. In the kitchen, she filled a glass of water from a pitcher as silently as if Gert were not in her usual place, moving her pen across paper.

"We missed you last night, Chrissy."

"You went to the casino?"

"No. Tom and I came back here after dinner. We sat in the

moonlight. Not too close to the pool," she added.

Christine made an effort to nod and headed back upstairs.

"Wait a minute," Gert commanded. "Tom said I should mention it to you, your drinking. Bad for your liver."

"Tom ought to know." Christine felt irritation beneath her fatigue and her queasiness.

"Tom's a big guy, whereas you're light as a feather. Think what it does to the rest of you. Your heart, your soul."

Only Gert would mention anyone's soul. "And you? What about you?"

"What about me?" Gert had just perfected on paper a fish as angelic as the one in the aquarium.

"Your phobia. Last night had to be hell for you. Elena made it worse."

"Just a passing show, Chrissy," Gert said, her hands on her hips. "Sure, Elena was callous, but what do you expect, with her gothic upbringing? Poor thing. And let's face it: my fear of the water is odd."

"It's more than odd, Gert. Your tears last night were real."

"My problem is water; pure H_2O. You're the one with the disease. Do something about it."

Christine felt the stab of truth, which Gert was so capable of sinking into her heart. In her stupor the night before, she was the one who might have drowned, the rum and gin working her over, sending her under. She had zero confidence that she could change her life, though. Not that morning. Why wasn't Gert's moral compass pointing at Elena for being so casually cruel and at Gert herself for not respecting her own fear and making a fool of herself? This many years later, Christine had sat through enough AA meetings to have heard lots of people embrace their worst moments, unbowed by ridicule. Gert's lack of embarrassment was probably part of the "realness" Tom admired in her from the start. Their marriage had survived, at any rate, much to everyone's surprise.

At the time, however, Christine strode out of the kitchen, confounded and infuriated, to pack for the flight home. Upstairs she found Geoff zipping up his backpack. She went over to the closet to rummage for her own few things and the blue dress. Where had it gone?

"You threw it out the window," Geoff said.

"God, what a mess I am."

"No, you're sweet." He kissed the back of her neck, as she looked down into the alley below their room. Something lay at the bottom, a patch that was dark and wet.

"Want me to go get it?" Geoff asked.

They went down together. The alley was a straight shot between adobe walls. Christine crouched over the dress, which looked something like a downed kite, badly torn and gritty.

"You ripped it on the railing on the way up to bed, remember? Right after that last nightcap."

She shook her head. She didn't remember.

"You nearly fell down the stairs, so it was a good thing. The belt broke your fall. I caught you, and then you went to sleep."

His voice came light as air; no judgment, no disgust. It was up to Christine to feel those things if she wanted to or not. She gathered the dress in her arms.

"Yuck, it's so dirty, honey." Gently, Geoff pulled it from Christine's hands and dropped it into a trash can in the alley.

"I took it from a closet in the master bedroom," she told him.

"You chose well. It did look good on you."

"I guess we'll have to pay for it."

"Nah." He shooed away her concern with a wave of his hand. "I wouldn't worry about it, Chrissy. Nobody's going to care."

Christine had wanted to tell Elena about the dress, but Elena had something else on her mind.

"Take a walk with me."

The invitation came as a surprise. Elena had been distracted most of the week. She looked harried and drawn, no longer as fresh and vital as she had been in Ann Arbor. Together they went down to the beach and walked along the shore. Salt on their lips and seawater on their skin allowed them to ignore that they were people, let alone women. Perhaps it was a creature's comfort that Elena sought when she found Christine's hand and whispered in her ear,

"I'm pregnant."

Christine drew back. She let go of Elena's hand. "Are you happy?"

"What do you think, silly? Yeah, we're a little freaked out, but we're lucky."

Once she returned home, Christine learned for certain. She, too, was carrying a being in and out of that swimming pool in Old San Juan: all that liquid, interior and exterior, sloshing and washing inside and out, holding their child, Geoff's and hers, in suspension. The miscarriage had come as a tremendous relief. She wasn't ready to give birth to anything but her own life. She used to wonder if the loss had weighed on Geoff. Either way, it was probably inevitable, his wandering away from their marriage, amiable as ever, no looking back.

Loss had followed loss. Recovery was as abrupt as it was mysterious. Somehow the desire returned to clean up her act; to follow through on her faceoff with the little Canadian, who had pulled her out of the pool; to endure it all naked and clean, her ordinary life. She went back to school. She built a business. She learned how to glide from Point A to Point Z with fewer missteps. She no longer lived in the slipstream of an artist, whether it was Gert's or Geoff's.

So here she was, on her way to a place she never thought she would revisit, the place where her life had broken in two. Tonight she could afford to fly business class, and there was no hippie sundress in her luggage. She often was the best dressed person in the room. She was making this second trip again at the invitation of Karl and Elena. Christine hadn't kept in touch with them much over the years, but she knew that they had done well for themselves. Somewhere in the hills outside San Juan, they had found a midcentury-modern to fix up and had sought her out, wanting her professional advice and willing to pay for it. Karl's successful career confirmed American clout but not necessarily anything crooked. She remembered the taller happy hour Canadian describing business on the island as "absolutely above aboard and absolutely low down." No need to break the law to make a killing when the system was crafted to help you do just that. She liked to think Karl's integrity had remained high on that low bar.

As the plane neared the island, the prospect of what lay before her stirred her: a chance to work on a neglected old beauty of a house; to spend time with Karl, whom she had always liked and whose moneyed comfort probably had helped to stay nice; to study the trove of Caribbean art that he and Elena had amassed, which was bound to be exceptional. Elena was so good with her oyster knife, as Geoff once said, deftly excising the innards of art. She was also a past master of "clique paradise," which was how Gert described the island after she and Tom visited again. "Who's cool and who are your friends? The answers matter more than they do in high school, and Elena has the right ones."

Still, Christine felt more unsettled than she usually did when she was starting a new project.

The pool inside the villa came to mind again. The eternity she sensed in the water, cradling birth and death and rebirth, calmed and reassured her. Yet the pool itself was not as crisp in memory as it used to be. This second visit to the island would bring new images. Some of them might overlay this one she clung to for consolation and cause it to dissolve. No, she couldn't let that happen. There must be a way to enliven what had begun to fade. And what if some remnant were to resurface of her youthful self, who had wanted to ascend to the sky, who loved the feel of blue silk against her skin, who hadn't yet grown up? Was there a way to reclaim some of her spirit without a rum punch? Did she want to? Was that another reason to come back here—to search for whole cloth, if mended with embroidery? The sudden rush of exhilaration surprised her as she felt for her carry-on bag. Inside she had stowed a Peruvian blanket, a housewarming gift for Karl and Elena. She lifted it out of the tissue paper and traced its intricate pattern with her fingers; a quick fix for her nerves.

Their French Mothers

For Alan Pearce

L ouise's hair was the color of a copper beech leaf, her gardener was telling them at her memorial service, longwindedly underway in the overheated solarium at her home in Connecticut. What hokum, Alex thought. Her hair had been frizzy and undoubtedly dyed for almost as long as he could remember, which took him back some fifty years, a boy on the cusp of puberty, marooned by his older sisters to greet the first arrivals at their parents' frequent dinner parties. Once allowed to escape, he ran upstairs. Yet there were times when he and Louise spoke in the hall. He remembered her eyes: their shrewd intelligence, their undeceived view of life. Louise wasn't beautiful like his mother, Hélène, but she was as formidable: another French woman on her game. The two had been the dearest of friends.

"Bien élevé," Alex had flown up from Washington to escort Hélène here today, which was why he sat beside her now, both of them uncomfortable in their folding chairs. He didn't

visit often. The trips he and Carol used to make so their kids could know the grandparents were a thing of the past. The kids lived on the West Coast now, with half-grown kids of their own. After Dad died, almost a decade ago, Alex felt less desire to visit and could blame a heavy workload in Washington. After he retired, he took refuge in habit.

It was his sisters who were all in. They had continued to live nearby and seemed to anticipate Hélène's every need, particularly after she entered her nineties and began to slip a little. They would have escorted Mom here today but for functions with their own grandkids, who seemed to preoccupy them less than Hélène did. All the more reason to attend the basketball tournament and the school play than to sit here at a funeral. If they resented his living at a distance, they hid it well. Certainly he was in their debt.

Eventually, of course, Mom would reach the point where there would be little more for his sisters to do but wait until life and death crossed like ocean currents. About this wait, however, nothing was said. To keep up the pretense that life would roll on without end was the thing to do, and Hélène led the way on that score.

Spending time with her today, he was struck by her appetite for life, stronger than his own. Something in the natural order of things, he sensed, would get the upper hand before he knew it, and bag him. Not so, Mom. He had a hunch that she would enter into the mysterious process of dying only when she wanted to, and then proceed with her usual high marks. Maybe she thought so, too. A conquistador of the self she had always been.

He didn't love her the way he had loved his dad, with open, easy affection. His love for her mainly took the form of admiration and respect. To wait for her death made him anxious. Sometimes during their telephone conversations, he would silently beg her. Please go ahead and take the plunge, so that I can stop bracing myself for your disappearance. She didn't seem to guess how he felt, but he wasn't certain. She might. Yet why shouldn't she live on, with no question raised as to the passage of time? Was it because he hated long good-byes? He put off calling her, he had to admit. Yet he carted her around on his back, her weight in his head and in his heart. Detach, his Buddhist friends would tell him, so that you may embrace her. Still, he couldn't. He went on feeling that he owed her more than he could give.

Mercifully, the gardener's tribute turned out to be the last, and the memorial service came to a close. Louise's daughter, Laura, stood up to welcome everyone to the reception.

"Let's walk down to the living room now, shall we? My mother loved to entertain there."

Alex remembered Laura playing "Blue Suede Shoes" on her guitar as a teenager. At seventy, she was still a youthful figure in a leopard-patterned blouse and form-fitting slacks.

Mom took hold of his hand and, with a tug, urged him to lead her out ahead of the crowd. They knew the house well. Louise and Ralph had settled here after the war and raised

Laura not far from where Dad and his own war bride had raised Alex and his sisters. It was unlikely they would come here again, he thought. Ralph had died a few years before, after a battle with cancer, torturously waged, and Laura lived on the other side of the country, a tenured professor at a great university.

As they entered the living room, Alex and Hélène came to a halt, transfixed. Louise was there to greet them—or at least a video freeze-frame was—of her face projected onto the walls.

Hélène nudged him in the ribs. "She's a guest at her own funeral," she sneered, clearly amused.

Well, Mom was cynical like that. For Alex it was a pleasant jolt to see Louise, as brimful of life as ever. Then the walls went blank, and her face vanished.

The room had been cleared of most furniture, but a buffet table stood at the ready under a bank of windows. Hélène sat down in one of the few upholstered chairs pushed into a corner, while Alex crossed over to the table. He filled a plate for his mother, knowing she would eat little. As he turned toward her again, he saw her face light up. Laura was coming through the garden doors behind him. Her hand grazed his sleeve as she passed him by and headed over to Hélène.

The constant changes in his mother's features this afternoon were fascinating. At times, confusion dimmed her beautiful eyes, filming them over. Then suddenly they gleamed beneath the markings of age, the way they had just now. Sometimes her smile looked pasted on to mask her struggle to keep up with the flow of talk around her. Yet a certain command remained. People had always paid court to her. It was her due. Not that she ever asked. Silent self-possession radiated like a radio wave.

She surprised him, then, by rising to her feet to greet Laura, offering her the compliment of her esteem, or perhaps her self-assertion, despite her weakened state and her fatigue. The two women exchanged kisses, cheek to cheek.

As he approached with the plate and a Perrier for his mother, Laura looked up at him with mild affection and mild disdain. "Pour me a glass of wine, won't you, Alex? Hélène and I need a tête–à–tête before the room fills up."

Laura had never stood on ceremony, of course. She had her mother's brains and her power of presence but didn't look like Louise. Laura was tall and blonde with froggy eyes in a pretty face. She was edgier than her mother, too. Her highhanded charm brought back lots of little moments when he had been the youngest in the mix of kids thrown together at holiday gatherings. How bold she had been and how cool, the way she made her voice sound black when she sang the blues in his parents' living room. His sisters never liked her much. Her elementary guitar licks were hard to forgive. They were serious musicians, who wouldn't have been caught dead playing for the old fogies in Brooks Brothers' sports jackets at those long-ago parties. Those parties: they were brave fronts against harsh realities, Dad used to joke. He and Mom had been awfully good at throwing them: rich cassoulets and cabernet, bravado and banter. Vietnam could slip the minds of the guests who agonized about the war.

Alex took his time pouring the wine and let himself observe the tête–à–tête discreetly at a distance. Laura's usual swagger was gone as she stood there with his mother. She looked almost girlish now; earnest, anxious, and worn as she spoke to Hélène, who might be like a second mother to her, an only child, now an orphan. To have to stage this memorial must have taken its toll on her. He was used to seeing her in command. In auditoriums, where he had heard her lecture from time to time, she provoked you to sense if not exactly grasp the essential ideas that lay above and beyond what she had to say with her usual verve on certain aspects of language she had reflected on for years. Never one to shrink from the hard work of thinking, high-octane Laura.

Out the living room window lay Louise's garden, much admired, with a pond on the far edge of an acre of landscape. Maybe Mom would like a stroll before they headed back to her condo? They could make their peace with Louise's death, striding along in silence; no need to force chat the way they did long distance. Their telephone conversations had long ago taken a certain form. There was world news to dissect, and the economy to treat like the weather, with a nod to the latest updraft or downturn in the market. Family matters might be mentioned, especially if someone had a problem. Art should have been a topic, what with her long curatorial career and his postretirement passion to paint.

His first cityscapes in oil had been easy to admire and easy to forget. Gradually, however, his pictures had grown bolder, simpler, and stronger in color and line, which seemed to satisfy viewers enough to want to actually buy them, rather than just congratulate him for his late-blooming talent. As stylized as these recent paintings were, they seemed to carry a few flecks of life whose transference to the canvas seemed miraculous. He would have liked to talk to Mom about the process. She knew so much about art, but he knew better than to bring up the topic. Mom changed the subject whenever he started to speak about something he cared about, or had accomplished, which admittedly must have bored her in years gone by, given the bureaucratic intricacies of his career at State. Now he realized it made no difference what the subject matter was. She distanced herself from any topic that got him excited enough to want to engage her.

Guests could be heard, trooping down the hall, as Alex handed a glass of sauvignon blanc to Laura. Quickly the living room filled to capacity, and the mood quickened as Louise's face suddenly flashed up on the walls again. This time her face was moving. The glimpse Alex and Hélène had caught earlier turned out to be only a trial run for the full viewing at hand. Everyone turned to watch.

Louise seemed to smile directly out at them, although what she really was doing in the video was greeting other guests, who had come to celebrate her birthday in the Dordogne region of southern France the previous June in the house where she was born and where she vacationed every summer. Few in the living room had made it to that party, including Hélène, for whom a transatlantic flight was out of the question. Now they were getting a taste of what they had missed. Laura's husband, Todd, had swept across that summer afternoon with his camera and his own observant eye.

On the walls, golden light fell on fresh leaves at the back of the old stone house and on the polished surfaces of the venerable furniture inside. Cooler light glinted on the ribbons of the wrapped gifts that sat in small pyramids at the foot of Louise's chair and on the silver and glass and porcelain on the dining room table, set for lunch. Then the guests came into view, embracing and chattering, before they receded into silhouettes against the backlit windows. On Louise, the camera shed radiance. She was everywhere with everyone: kissing the newly arrived, clinking her champagne flute against theirs, going into lunch, blowing out an impressive if inadequate number of candles, and easing finally into her armchair to open gifts, which her granddaughter handed up to her, one by one.

The French party flowed on as smoothly as the little stream of water at the edge of the property. On the living room walls, at least, the whole summer lay ahead, just as it had for many years, a happy prospect. The sun set pink and peach as the last party guests waved at Todd's camera and departed. From the threshold of Louise's birthplace, the beauty of the surrounding landscape shone in a final frame.

"A perfect death," someone murmured as the walls went blank.

Agreement rippled through the living room. Everyone knew what had happened next: Louise went up to bed that night and died in her sleep.

Yes, the way Louise had died could be envied, Alex thought. All the essentials had been there: love and beauty, harmony and contentment. Wasn't it a little too idyllic, though? Alex didn't think he would like to die oblivious, even in pastoral France. He would rather be awake to his own death and to press a human hand as he went.

Laura hugged Hélène again and crossed over to the buffet table. She faced the room with a slight smile as the crowd of guests turned toward her expectantly.

"A perfect death, someone just said. Yes, it was," she agreed, nodding out at people well on in years, who had known Louise for a long time "Still, it's my mother's life I want you to know more about before we all go home today." Then she launched into a story with the ease of the seasoned lecturer she was, slowly pacing along the length of the buffet table as she spoke.

"As most of you know, Louise met Ralph in Paris in 1945, after his discharge from the U.S. Army. He arranged to stay on to study economics for his doctoral dissertation. What you probably don't know is that my mother was married to another man at the time. She didn't know it either; she thought she was a widow. In 1942, her husband, Jean, was caught working on the black market and was arrested. Louise could find out nothing more. The general assumption was that, like many others in his place, he had been put on a transit to work at one of the forced labor camps in the east. The war went on. The years went by. Louise had no reason to believe that she would ever hear from Jean again, especially because she knew the truth: Jean had done more than buy and sell on the black market. He had worked for the resistance, and resisters weren't sent to labor camps; they were executed.

"Somehow he survived years of hard labor at a camp in Poland. In the chaos of the liberation, he was set out on the road, but it was more than a year before he was strong enough to travel any great distance. Eventually, he knocked on the door of his old apartment in Paris. Louise was there to open up to a man, who only slowly grew recognizable, the remains of her husband. She took him in and nursed him, little by little, back to some level of health, never to regain the strength he once had, but he would live, as shocked to be alive as she was to have him reappear.

"She broke things off with Ralph of course. Their parting was bitterly sad; another casualty of war. Each of them understood. It was now my mother's task to pick up where life had left off years before. Jean set out on the long haul of recovery. For hours, he sat on the sofa or at the kitchen table, staring into space, seeing and hearing and feeling things Louise couldn't see or hear or feel.

"Months went by. Mother wasn't able to live up to the standard she set for herself. To live as Jean's wife felt false. During the war, she had grieved like his widow. Gradually, she began to heal. She found someone to love, who loved her too. This new love rose out of the ashes. She couldn't bring herself to kill it now. One day after their midday meal, she folded her napkin and called on her reserve of courage.

"Jean fought to keep her, but he was weaker than he used to be. She arrived at Ralph's door with a black eye, which made it easier to file for divorce. Ralph completed his studies, and they moved to the States. Well, you know the rest of her story. Most of you here today shared it in one way or another."

Laura stood silent for a moment, letting the guests in the living room take in what they had never known about Louise. So many of them looked fragile with age, Alex noticed. Yet there they stood. Then she spoke again.

"My mother told me about Jean only a few days before she died. It was clear he was very much on her mind. She told me she respected his bitterness. What's more, his terrible personal losses were woven into her life. It was his tragedy that led to her future happiness, she wanted me to know."

The caterers began to pass around trays, filled with flutes of champagne. Laura took one and raised it in a toast.

"To Louise and Jean," she called out. "To live and die as well as my mother did can't make up for pain and desolation; it can't undo injustice. Yet I believe the beauty of her life did honor to the heroism of his."

"*Mais oui*," someone called back softly.

There was muttered assent. A few people clapped. Others smiled as Laura waded into the room to chat a little with guests preparing to say goodbye. The nonchalance Alex sensed all around him came as a surprise. Laura's story seemed to have been digested in one easy gulp. Was it because most of these men and women had been young themselves during the war? Louise's story was undoubtedly one of so many, each wrenching in its own way.

How was Mom taking it in, this outing of her dear friend by her own daughter? He turned to look at Hélène, who gave him a smirk, her eyes full of bright mischief. Oh, a typical reaction then. To her, it only made sense to make light of human weakness. But wasn't the point of a memorial service to bring Louise into positive focus before she faded from mind? Why mar her fairy tale ending, so beautifully projected earlier on the living room walls? Why not just stick to nice things, even inane things, like the gardener, who had said Louise had hair the color of a copper beech leaf, not that she was someone who walked out on a concentration camp survivor? Yes, there had been a perfect death. It was the death Louise conveniently believed in long enough to fall in love with Ralph. Alex looked out again at the landscape. He was sorry he hadn't gone out there and missed Laura's speech.

It was she who sidled up and nudged him gently, catching him unawares. "I see you're interested in the garden. Want to take a walk?"

Alex glanced again at Hélène. She didn't look ready to leave. In fact, she was talking with a couple who didn't seem to mind that they had to bend down low to converse with her, seated in the upholstered chair.

Outside, Laura led the way along the ornamental beds, somber this late in October. When they reached the pond, they stopped and stood side-by-side. On the far property line, the copper beech leaves shimmered. So there were the trees, after all, too far out of range to be seen from the living room window.

"I met him once," Laura said. "Jean."

Alex turned to look at her, but she kept her eyes on the pond, her arms tight across her chest.

"During my first visit to France," she went on.

"When was that?"

"Oh, I was ten, so it would have been 1956. Mother and I took a train south to visit what remained of her family, an aunt and uncle, in a village far from her own in the Dordogne. It was late autumn, not a pretty time of the year. When we arrived, quite a little crowd had gathered to meet us: more cousins than mother knew she had; friends and neighbors, too, possibly, but no children that I recall. Courbet might have liked to move forward in time and south in location to paint the scene: everything rustic, somber inside and out, enough brown and gray for his taste.

"Someone set me down in a chair near the fireplace. The

heat and the sound of adults talking made me drowsy. I
wasn't used to French, except with my mother. Then someone else came into the room. He wasn't a big man. He had
a long nose, which reminded me of a rodent's. He was furi-
ous, seething. He got into my mother's face and then he
screamed. '*Putain! Espèce de putain! Et tu oses rentrer ici. Salope!*'
I only figured out that he was calling her a 'whore' and a 'slut'
when I got older.

"The sounds he made were frightening enough all by
themselves: so loud and harsh that at first I thought he was
speaking German, and there was a hysterical edge to his
voice, which made me feel he was about to go completely
out of control. Another man took hold of his arm, and got
him out of the room. The silence he left behind was just as
dramatic. You could practically hear the dust stirring. The
motes in the window light seemed to tremble. The room was
an old-fashioned salon, a perfect place to view a corpse. I
looked across at my mother. She didn't look at me or anyone.
She just sat there, slumped forward, as if she had been hit
by a truck, which in a way she had been, and then I burst
into tears.

"A teenaged girl hustled me out into the kitchen, where
she set me down at the table and patted my hands gently,
trying to calm me down. Then she stepped away to slice
a fresh cake. I was greedy for the taste of something that
smelled so delicious, but my stomach churned. I could hear
the adults start up again in the front room, buzzing like
insects. The girl gave me a glass of fresh cow's milk, which I

ran outside into the yard to vomit. Of the man and why he had screamed into my mother's face nothing was said."

"You didn't ask?"

"Oh, I must have," she said. "But it didn't matter. The answers I received were the kind children usually receive. The man was sad and a little bit touched in the head. What had happened was just one of those things. On the train back to Paris, my mother was totally lost to me, lost in her thoughts. She looked so small and shrunken, as tiny as a bird. I remember I touched her hand, and she let me leave my fingers there on top of hers. She didn't usually like me to touch her.

"I don't know why Jean was there in the front parlor that day. Was he as shocked to see my mother as she was to see him? It's possible her relatives invited him there, out of spite. They weren't shy about their resentment of Mother for leaving them all behind. As far as I know, there were no more visits after that one miserable reunion.

"But she did make peace with Jean, eventually. Ralph knew, even encouraged their reconciliation, she told me. Maybe they sent Jean some money? He didn't live a long life, not surprisingly. Mother visited him in a nursing home in Paris once, where she found him wheelchair-bound but lucid. He asked her to name with him the birds outside his window and the fruit trees. Her life, he told her, defied the wretched ones and made it possible to believe in goodness. A noble sentiment, I know, but mother was grateful. Anyway, that's what she told me."

"Well, he had been in the resistance. An idealist, right?"

"Apparently. I was trying to capture what he said to my mother in my toast today: happy lives can comfort those whose own lives are unhappy."

Alex nodded. "Living well is the best revenge, even if somebody else is doing it?"

"That might have been a better toast."

"Oh, I don't know. People seemed to like what you did say."

"People?" she hooted. "What about you?"

"I'm not an idealist."

"Doesn't matter," she said flatly. "Tell me what you thought."

"So I wondered why you told us about Jean at all. Your mother had to jilt a broken man to claim her good life."

Laura stared at him. "That's bold of you, Alex. I thought tact and diplomacy were your game."

"I ask, because I was fond of your mother. Why not protect her good image?"

"Truth is beauty, dear. You know that."

A rough path ran around the pond, and Laura started along it in a hurry. Then she slowed, seeming to relent a little. "What you say is true of course. My mother claimed her life. I leave it to others to judge."

"I know you can take tough questions," he said, following in her footsteps. "I've admired your toughmindedness ever since I was a kid."

She laughed. "Not at all," she said over her shoulder. "I'm not tough. Not nearly as tough as my mother was. Or yours is. Neither one of us is, now are we? Were they tough by nature? Were they raised to be iron? Or was it living through the war when they were teenagers? The point is: we aren't like them. We're soft. We know hardship and injustice third hand, if we suffer at all."

"Yes, and we softies tend to romanticize suffering, wouldn't you say? Isn't that what you're doing, making it noble?"

She came to a halt, almost causing him to run into her. "Another low blow, Alex, but I'm guilty of just the opposite. I'm saluting a happy ending, which sounds foolish. Only we would find it hard to live without the possibility of one, don't you think? My mother gave happiness her best shot. She was lucky. She came closer to it than most."

"I don't doubt it, Laura. Honestly, I was just thinking of how the point of most memorials is to at least protect, if not burnish, the reputation of the departed."

"You prefer protocol, of course. Well, my mother doesn't need her secrets now," Laura flung at him, red faced, completely dismissive. "I'll tell you one more. Just before she died. We were settling into what we thought would be another wonderful summer in the old house in her village. After we had been there a few days, I came downstairs one morning to find her caught up in memories. She sat me down with an intent look on her face. That was when she told me the story you just heard inside. Only there was a little bit more to it than that."

Laura's voice trailed off then. She seemed to be in search of words, not as sure of herself as she usually was. When she spoke again, however, she sounded quite assured.

"This is what she said to me: 'I left Jean just as he was beginning to regain his strength, ready to believe life was worth living again. He lost everything. Especially you.' She looked me in the eye, waiting for me to understand, until it dawned on me what she was telling me."

"What a bombshell to drop on you, Laura."

She nodded. "It was a twist I could have done without, but there it is. Probably she believed she owed me and her granddaughter the truth; health, genetic history. She put herself at risk, not knowing how I would feel about her choices. My mother never cried. She cried when she told me. She was defiant, though: 'What I did is unforgiveable,' she said. 'Yet I would do it again.'

Laura turned to look at Alex. "I was glad, because Ralph will always be 'dad' to me."

"So why did you make a toast to Jean instead?"

"Oh, I wanted to honor him—or to romanticize him, if you prefer. No one else needed to know who he was to me."

"No one else knew?"

Laura shook her head. "My mother said she never told anyone."

"Not even Ralph?"

"I don't think so. I couldn't bring myself to ask. She left Jean soon after he began to make love to her again. She couldn't take it, she said, but she was sure I was Jean's."

Alex winced. Laura was right. He did prefer protocol and a memorial service that would have burnished the fixed images of people he had known such a long time.

"I told Todd after Mother died. And your mother."

"My mother?"

"Yes. I called her recently, after I started to think about what I might say here today. I wanted her to know first."

"How did she take it?"

"She hardly reacted at all. 'My dear friend is dead,' she said. 'That's all I need to know.'"

Alex sighed. "You know my mother. She may feel things deeply, but she'll give you little to go on."

"Unlike you, Alex. You're quick to express an opinion." Laura looked at him gravely. "I dragged you out here, because it matters to me, your being the person closest to my mother's closest friend, except your sisters maybe. You say you were fond of Louise. So please allow yourself to know who she was without judging so quickly. Your memories give you something to build on now that your understanding of her life is more complete."

He nodded in agreement but still would rather not have known. Louise was as fuzzy to him now as her hair used to be. The woman he used to greet at his parents' parties half a century ago was the Louise he would remember. Her kind interest had flustered and flattered him, an interest he wasn't used to receiving as a child.

"Louise's hair was the color of a copper beech leaf," he said. "That was the last thing somebody said about her in the solarium. Remember?"

"Yes," Laura answered. "George worked with my mother on this garden for years."

"It occurs to me now that it was your mother's mind that was like a copper beech leaf: so bright and abiding."

"That's a nice thought, Alex," Laura nodded. "You are sensitive, aren't you?" She looked more closely at him, as if she were taking his measure. "I'm beginning to think you're what I call a 'fine flower.'"

"What's that supposed to mean?"

"You blossom when the world outside your door is fat and happy, in dirt well fertilized with the decay of lives that might be glad to know they served such a purpose. You wouldn't bloom in any other place or time. So paint away."

"Paint?"

"Yes, paint," she said, and moved her hand back and forth as if she held a brush and was dabbing with it furiously.

"I was unaware you knew I did."

"Hélène told me."

"Oh."

"Don't look so surprised. She has always sung your praises, and now she's especially pleased to have you take up something so central to her own interests."

It was true he should know better than to be surprised by Mom. He never knew what she was thinking. Yet he found it difficult to imagine her singing anyone's praises, certainly not his.

"You're a fine flower, too, aren't you," he retorted, "with your rarified investigations into arcane subjects?"

"Yes, I am," she smiled, with her hands on her hips. "I too am soft."

"No you're not."

"Well, I'm worn out then." Her smile turned weary.

"So we fine flowers haven't inherited longevity any more than toughness from our mothers?"

"No, you probably wouldn't have survived what Jean went through. Maybe not even come out the other side the way my mother did or your mother did. Softness has its worth, though," she said, seeming to have sunk into her own thoughts.

"Not in art," he said. "'You gotta suffer to sing the blues.' The 'brutality of fact' and so on."

"Not always," she insisted. "The beautiful and the innocent, the fragile and the ephemeral can be just what we look for when we suffer, their very softness a rallying cry. To Jean, my mother's later life was a work of art that gave the devil the finger, I think."

"Okay. A fine flower or two can serve a purpose now and then, I suppose," Alex said, because he could see how much she needed to believe Jean had been happy to see Louise happy, that her good life vindicated his.

"Don't worry," she added, almost in a whisper. "Your mother will die someday."

"What? Why bring that up?" She had caught him off guard again.

"Hélène weighs on you."

"What makes you say that?"

"She's a force of nature, Alex."

True enough. Alongside his mother's elusiveness lay her magnetism. Her power might be banked, yet it was potent. He resisted her pull, and he probably always would, so he could call his life his own.

He made the slightest bow. "And I shall miss her."

"Mais oui."

He let out a deep sigh, relaxing into the liberation of being understood at least a little bit, for better and for worse. Laura was something else, wasn't she, breaking with protocol, breaking molds? All he could do was to give in to his desire to kiss her cheek and grasp her hand as they walked back to the house.

Inside, he glanced across at Hélène. He would have liked to paint her as she was, there in the moment, in the chair, in her element. He wondered if he had the skill to work later from memory, or the guts, really. Before he could look away, she caught him in a glance, smiling at him as if she saw him for who he was.

ACKNOWLEDGMENTS

Stories are conceived out of the daydreams of writers. They come to life with the help of generous first readers, their midwives. During its long gestation period, this book was extremely fortunate to have been read by Marina France, Karen Ruckman, Marcia Sartwell, Sam Soopper, and Robin Underdahl, whose insights, questions, and encouragements helped me better see and understand where the stories needed to go—and they seemed to believe I could get them there.

Above all, I thank Steve France, my partner. These stories would not exist without his thoroughgoing critique and imaginative flair.

For permission to use Lisa Neher's vibrant painting *Tuscany* on the book's cover, I thank Lisa's husband, Roger Miller. For her photograph of the painting, I thank Karen Ruckman, a colleague and friend of the late artist.